A
CONSPIRACY
OF GENES

Mark de Castrique

BellaRosaBooks

BellaRosaBooks

A CONSPIRACY OF GENES
ISBN 978-1-933523-35-4
2008 Reprint Edition by Bella Rosa Books

Previously Published in the U.S.A. by Quiet Storm Books. First Edition: January 2006; ISBN 0977007081.

Printed in the United States of America on acid-free paper.

Cover by INDIEVISION; Tony Elwood and Rob Hall

BellaRosaBooks and logo are trademarks of Bella Rosa Books

10   9   8   7   6   5   4   3   2   1

DEDICATION

This story is a work of fiction. However, the tremendous work of the caregivers at Levine Children's Hospital at Carolinas Medical Center is reality. Thousands of children and their families are living testimony to the commitment and kindness that radiates from these healthcare professionals.

This book is dedicated to them and the children they serve.

ACKNOWLEDGMENTS

I am grateful to Dr. Mark West of the University of North Carolina at Charlotte for his guidance and support. Thanks to my agent Linda Allen for her constant encouragement. My daughters, Melissa and Lindsay, contributed the youthful perspective of their suggestions. I'm also indebted to Rob Hall and Tony Elwood for creating a wonderful cover, to Earl Staggs for his eagle editorial eye, and to Rod Hunter and Bella Rosa Books for this edition. Most importantly, thanks to the Carolinas HealthCare Foundation and The Children's Miracle Network for giving me the opportunity to work with such wonderful children who receive care in Levine Children's Hospital.

THE PRESENT

1

My name is Gene. I ask for your patience. I know you'll become annoyed and irritated that I don't explain everything at once. Trust me. Had I not uncovered the truth, bit by bit, fact by fact, I'd have dismissed the final revelation as the delusion of madmen or a trap set by those who trick the gullible.

I myself have never been gullible, except perhaps in believing my own senses, trusting my intuition, and relying upon my intelligence. This morning I look in the mirror and see the youthful face of a nineteen-year-old boy. But the eyes have aged, no longer bright with innocence. People say I have sad eyes. Those who don't know me proclaim I'll be a poet when I grow older. What I have to say can't be captured in lines, no matter how free the verse. My story is a mystery, a discovery, and a coming of age in a manner that even now seems unbelievable to me.

And so I set words to paper, not so much so you can believe what has happened to me, but so you can prepare for what will happen to you, you who are eager to make your own way. This is a story about my past and your future because the two are linked, and what I experienced by accident, you might someday experience by choice.

But first you must choose to come back with me. I'd just turned seventeen during the summer before my senior year in high school . . .

THE PAST

2

. . . and although I didn't have to be at work until nine that Monday morning, I pulled my Toyota Corolla into Employee Parking Lot B at seven-twenty. My dad had gotten up at six to catch a flight for a business trip to Chicago. He was a banker like half the other fathers and mothers in Charlotte. I'd set my alarm to join him for breakfast since he'd be gone a week.

Breakfast together had become a habit begun when we would go to visit Mom in the hospital. Afterwards, he'd go to work and I'd go to school. Mom died in the spring, leaving her husband and only child to continue breakfast together.

The trips to the hospital continued as well, only now I worked a summer job in the Child Life department. I spent my days on the children's floor as a combination nurse's assistant and on-demand per-former. My hobbies of magic, juggling, and silly song writing found a ready audience among those young-sters whose days would be filled with pills and pain, pokes and prods, tests and transfusions. I was a break in the waiting and worrying, the familiar friend or big brother who never hurt them and who always smiled even when looking into the face of a kid who would never get better, who would never go home.

I got out of my car and felt the furnace called July hit me with an early morning blast of heat and humidity. The day promised to be a scorcher. I clipped my nametag to my shirt pocket. My photograph cruelly captured the dopey expression of one bewildered by the harsh flash of a digital camera placed a foot away. All photographers in departments of personnel and driver's licenses must attend a school for taking bad pictures. At least my name was spelled right—Gene Adamson. The mistake was the M.D. after it. I didn't have Personnel correct it and I fantasized being the youngest doctor in Carolinas Medical Center.

I'd just reached in the back seat for my guitar case when a beep sounded behind me. Jeanne Everston wheeled her forest green Miata convertible into the adjacent spot and killed the engine. I must admit my early arrival wasn't to get to work before everyone else. Jeanne usually drove in around seven-thirty. If I could play doctor, Jeanne would be the patient of choice.

She'd moved from Colorado to Charlotte with her father in the middle of spring term and wound up sitting beside me in American History class.

Being able to fit in with high school students so late in the school year wasn't easy. And Jeanne was friendly but aloof in a way that seemed more self-confident and mature than snooty. She was also gorgeous and a disappointment to the senior guys who thought this new junior would be anxious to hang with one of the "hotties." Each in turn—the captain of the football team, the captain of the basketball team, the Senior Class President, and the boy whose father owned the Porsche dealership—was politely but clearly given the line: "I've got a boyfriend back in Denver."

As for me, I had a mother dying of a rare, incurable liver virus who needed and deserved my attention and didn't have the status of a sports star or "Mr. Personality." I did find Jeanne much more exciting to look at than maps of Robert E. Lee's campaigns or Sherman's March to the Sea.

Something about her was exotic—coal black hair, wide brown eyes, and a smooth complexion which seemed to shift from bronze to light cocoa depending upon the color of her clothes. I was too shy and intimidated and probably would have sat mute beside her for the rest of the term if Mr. Wallingford, our teacher, hadn't paired his two Gene/Jeannes together for our Civil War project. Maybe it made it simpler to call on us. "Hey, Gene/Jeanne, give us a progress report." Maybe he knew I was going through a tough time and thought Jeanne would boost my spirits.

Neither she nor I cared about the battle statistics or political beliefs of the North or South. We were both more interested in the common people and decided to do our project on the songs of the war.

Jeanne analyzed the lyrics for historical context, imagery, and impact on society. I researched the tunes—which ones were original, which came from earlier sources, and how they'd been handed down and transformed to this day. We worked separately at first, but then we met at the hospital cafeteria to share information. I would take a break from staying with Mom and find Jeanne at a table in the back corner, her note cards spread out in ordered groupings on the Formica top.

Jeanne spent several evenings a week at the hospital helping her father in the lab. Dr. Everston had come to Carolinas Medical Center as part of an exchange program in genetic research. He was a professor of bio-engineering who was taking a year's sabbatical from the University of Colorado to lend his expertise at the medical complex's Institute for Fertility and Reproductive Studies.

Biology wasn't my strength, but I gathered his work had to do with splitting chromosomes so infertile couples could have their own genetic code halved, then paired together in the nucleus of a human egg. The technique wasn't cloning, but genetic science carrying out nature's process of re-combining a father's and mother's DNA. Professor Everston's work wasn't the kind of conversation I pursued with Jeanne. My romantic fantasy and a clinical discussion of infertility didn't make a very good combination.

However, Jeanne and I made an A-plus combination in history class. She found great stories to set up the songs—stories drawn from obscure letters and diaries which brought the writers to life in a way no map or political essay could. For our presentation, I played my guitar and what started out as a dry assignment became a musical performance. Jeanne's voice was rich and clear, sounding older and filled with emotion that transported the entire class back to the war. Even Kevin Ferris, the class wiseguy, sat spell-bound during "Just Before the Battle, Mother." The applause broke spontaneously. It was great, but the smile Jeanne flashed at me was terrific.

That night I told Mom we even gave an encore. It was the last conversation she and I ever had.

That was months ago and since then, Jeanne and I had spent a good deal of time together, although I confess my mind was not always on music.

After she'd parked her Miata next to me, I stood up, guitar case in hand, and squinted against the morning sun.

Jeanne leaned from behind her steering wheel. "Going on tour without me?" She slipped a bright yellow scarf off her head and shook loose the mass of dark hair. My throat turned to sand.

"No," I croaked in a voice I thought I'd gotten rid of at age fourteen. "I'm doing some songs for the kids this morning. Say, can you come up at ten? Nobody sings 'Goober Peas' like you."

Jeanne laughed as she got out of the car. "Have you been tampering with verses again?"

"No, that one's silly enough."

The song, "Goober Peas," is about the Confederate soldiers' one nutritional provision: peanuts. Goober peas, as peanuts were called then, were all many of the starving men had to eat as the war-torn South limped to defeat. "I wish this war was over, when free from rags and fleas, we'd kiss our wives and sweethearts and gobble goober peas" goes the last verse. Jeanne and I sang that song in class as well. Unfortunately, Kevin Ferris started calling me

"Goober," and the name stuck. I hoped everyone forgot it over the summer.

Jeanne shook her head. "Any day but today. We've got a special event at lunch. A bio-chemist from Duke is presenting results of his research which may affect the work of my father. We're getting the lecture hall ready."

"Is your father speaking?"

"No, but he's on the panel that follows. It's open to the public and press. We expect mostly scientists and writers from medical journals. Not the kind of thing to attract the local TV stations, unless someone has a car crash on the way."

We walked through the employee entrance for the tower in which Jeanne worked. "So no big break-through," I said.

"Well, not the kind to make headlines. They have had success with recombining chromosomes in frog eggs."

"Might be tough telling a couple they've just had an eight-pound tadpole."

Jeanne didn't laugh. She shot me a look that made me wish I'd kept my mouth shut. "Some of the couples who come to the Institute would give anything to have a child. It's tough telling them there's nothing we can do."

"I'm sorry. I can imagine. I see parents who've been told there's nothing they can do to save the child they have."

Jeanne reached out and grabbed my arm. "Look. I'm too touchy. I admit it. I'd love to sing for the children some other time. Even 'Goober Peas.' Why don't you call me tonight? We can get together and practice."

Fortunately, this time I found my voice. "And if you need help today at lunch, it's no trouble. Any frog eggs I can carry?"

"No, but you can help me at the sign-in desk. The Institute likes to know who has an interest in their work. Can you come about eleven-thirty?"

"I think so. I'm in early now." I stopped at the elevator bank where Jeanne would ascend to the floor housing the Institute. "Should I meet you at the lecture hall?"

She pushed the up button and the door immediately opened. "Yes, I'll be in the lobby."

I tried to dazzle Jeanne with my wit. "Do we have to ask these attendees for a password?"

"Oh, yes. They have to know how you tell a boy chromosome from a girl chromosome."

I wished I'd paid more attention in biology so I could impress her with the right answer. "Something about an X or a Y?"

As the elevator door closed, Jeanne laughed. "We're the password. You pull down their genes."

3

I checked in at the nurses' station on the seventh floor where the Children's Hospital is located. Nurse Helen McBride, a no-nonsense woman in her fifties, looked up at me from her computer terminal, then glanced at the clock on the opposite wall.

"You're the early bird this morning, Gene. Anxious to get started on filing?"

When I wasn't transporting a child or entertaining in the playroom, I helped organize the volumes of patient records generated during the course of treatment.

"I've been asked to assist with a presentation in the lecture hall at lunch. I didn't want to get behind here."

"The lecture hall?" Nurse McBride asked. "Isn't that the speech by the professor from Duke? What's his name?"

I'd failed to ask Jeanne. I shrugged. "I don't remember. I'm not really interested in the topic."

Helen McBride slipped her reading glasses off her

nose and let them dangle from the neckchain against her starched uniform. She winked at me. "No, I didn't think you were interested in the topic, but I bet you haven't forgotten the name of Dr. Everston's daughter."

I hoped somewhere some medical scientist was working on a cure for blushing. I could feel even my ears going scarlet.

Helen McBride took pity. "That's all right, Gene. I'm assigning you to attend the lecture. And don't start on the filing yet. Katherine Thompson is going down for fluid relief at nine. She asked if you could see her first thing." The nurse nodded at the guitar case in my hand. "Something about a song."

I took a deep breath. "Thanks. And thanks for the lunch assignment. Is she still in seven-eleven?"

"Yes. They'll be moving her about eight-thirty."

I hoped seven-eleven would be a lucky room number. Katherine Thompson certainly needed some luck. Her heart was not growing properly. At age ten, she looked like she was six. The only hope left for her was a transplant. Her heart's ability to function had become so impaired that fluid built up around it, causing her stomach to appear distended. Relief came from tapping the chest cavity and draining it, a process neither pretty nor painless. She was a brave little girl. She shouldn't have needed a transplant because she'd stolen the heart from everyone on the hospital staff.

I paused in the hallway outside her open door. No sound came from within. Perhaps she'd fallen back asleep. The slightest activity quickly tired her and much of her day was spent in a series of naps. I peered around the doorframe and discovered her looking right at me. She'd been as true as any sentry posted on a watch tower. Her smile sprang across the room and captured me.

"Hey, Goober."

Kevin Ferris wasn't the only one to tag me with that nickname, but coming from little Katherine, "Goober" sounded like a title of royalty.

"Hey, yourself. I thought your momma told you not to call me that."

"She and Daddy ran down for breakfast. She wouldn't like the song I made up either."

"Song?"

"Yep." Katherine chuckled with excitement. The blue pallor of her face flushed slightly and she inched herself higher against the sheet of the inclined bed. "And you're gonna play it for me, Goober."

"I am not," I said, but I was already unfastening the clasps of my guitar case. "How can I play a song only you know?"

"It's 'Goober Peas,' " she said triumphantly, "except new and improved."

"And your mother wouldn't want to hear it."

"You gonna keep stalling till they come to drain me?"

"Okay, squirt. Let me see if I can find a key you'll almost sing in." I lifted my Ovation acoustical guitar from the case and pulled a chair closer to the bed. "What's the name of this masterpiece?"

Katherine smoothed her thin blonde hair as if preparing to step into the spotlight. "You'll see. Just start playing, Goober."

I ran a short intro up the bass strings, then began the melody for the verse. Katherine's whispery voice started late but caught up before the end of the first line.

"Sitting on my bedpan on a summer's day,

Waiting for the nurse to carry it away,

They give me lots of water, and say it's good for me,

But don't they understand it makes me have to pee."

Without missing a beat, she went into her chorus.

"Pee, pee, pee, pee, makes me have to pee,

I'm sitting on my bedpan because I have to pee."

I couldn't help but laugh, which was the reaction she wanted.

"Wait, there's a second verse."

"Why am I not surprised?" I slid the key from G to A just to tease her.

She stayed right with me.

"Now please don't get mad if you think I'm being crude,

The water ain't so bad, but you should taste the food,

The meat is burnt to ashes, and bugs swim in the soup,

I've gotten use to peein', but boy I hate to poop."

She flung her thin arms from side to side in time with the music and repeated the chorus.

"Pee, pee, pee, pee, makes me have to pee,

"I'm sitting on my bedpan because I have to pee."

"Katherine, whatever are you singing?" Mrs. Thompson stood just inside the door. Her short blond hair bounced as she shook her head with disapproval, but I could see the corners of her mouth twitching as she tried not to laugh.

Perky was the word that came to mind because she did her best to brighten everyone's day. If Katherine got the chance, she'd become the mirror image of her mother. Behind Mrs. Thompson stood her husband. While she was barely five feet tall, Mr. Thompson was over six. He leaned against the door-frame behind her, wearing a Carolina Panthers T-shirt and trying to hide his smile behind a jumbo cup of coffee.

"I know Gene didn't teach you that song," Mrs. Thompson said.

"No, he's not clever enough."

I laid my guitar back in the case. "I'm going to have the nurses store your bedpan in the freezer. Then we'll see who's clever when you're sitting on an ice cube."

"And it'll serve you right," Mrs. Thompson agreed. "Now let's get straightened up before they come for you."

The joy in little Katherine's face disappeared like a light switched off. I saw the fear flash for an instant before she could mask it.

"Okay, Mommy. Gene, will you help wheel me down?"

"Sure, on one condition."

"What's that?"

"No singing about peeing and pooping. If you get me fired, then who are you going to pick on?"

She stuck out her hand. "It's a deal."

I grasped the small fingers gently and the lightness of her smile made my own heart heavy.

4

Although I was anxious to meet Jeanne, the morning sped by quickly. I escorted some children to the rehab hospital for their physical therapy sessions, then did my magic show in the playroom for a group of four-to seven-year-olds.

In every performance, some kid always claimed to know how every trick was done. Today was no exception and David Louis Wilcox the Third no less said his father was a better magician because he could pull a quarter out of David's ear. I can't resist a challenge, even from a child who is recovering from appendicitis, and especially if the child seems arrogant or bossy. I'd already seen David take a puzzle away from a smaller kid.

"Well, a quarter's nothing," I said. "I'll find a fifty-cent piece. A whole half dollar."

With my pint-sized audience spellbound behind me, I crouched beside David Louis Wilcox the Third, grabbed his ear, and tugged. "Oops." I let the rubber ear I'd palmed expand between my fingers. "Looks like I pulled too hard."

The gasp from the children came only a second before David's wail. "My ear!" He clutched the side of his head and was doubly astonished to find nothing amiss. The other kids laughed at both the trick and David's panic. Tears flooded his eyes at the humiliation, but with visions of David Louis Wilcox the Second suing me and the hospital, I wrapped my arm around my victim and handed him the fake ear.

I met Jeanne at eleven-thirty inside the lecture hall. The facility consisted of a small stage on which was set a podium and a long table. The area for the audience held about one hundred fifty theater seats arranged in rows which sloped up to a projection booth at the rear of the room. Jeanne was fastening dark blue bunting to the front of the table. A technician from the audiovisual department uncoiled cable to the podium microphone. Four desk mikes were already in position on the table.

Jeanne saw me coming down the right-hand aisle. "Good, you made it. We're running behind."

"What can I do to help?"

"We need four chairs for the panel. They're backstage. You can't miss them because I've put a name card in each seat. You can roll them out here."

I climbed the short set of steps to the stage and walked behind the left wing. Five high-backed executive office chairs were lined up like airplanes on a runway. A stiff white placard rested on the seat cushion of the first four. I noticed Dr. Everston's name printed on one. The others were unfamiliar: Dr. Colbert, Dr. Pizzato, and Dr. Stamanovich. I wheeled the chairs out two at a time and centered each behind a microphone.

Jeanne arranged the names, then set out a pitcher of ice water and four glasses. "That should do it." She glanced at the technician standing behind the podium.

He vigorously flipped a toggle switch on and off, grumbling to himself.

"What's wrong?" Jeanne asked.

"The control for the screen is malfunctioning. Either that or the motor is broken."

We looked above the stage where the projector screen hung immobile in the grid.

Jeanne frowned. "We've got to have the slides, Mike."

Mike walked past us to the right wing. He pressed a green button mounted on the wall. A whir sounded overhead and the screen descended.

"It's the switch in the podium. We'll have to work it from here. Can one of you handle it? I've got to be in the booth covering sound and lighting."

I took a closer look. "Just push that button?"

"Well, it's not that easy. There are two buttons." Mike pointed to a red one above the green. I thought he was probably kidding, but some of these technoids were pretty humorless.

I ventured a guess. "The red one makes it go up?"

"Say, you studied this in school, didn't you?" He grinned and I realized he was human. "Okay, the guy at the podium—"

"Dr. Colbert," Jeanne interrupted.

"Whatever. He'll call for the slides. That's your cue."

I glanced at the stage. "So the screen's going to be in front of the table."

Jeanne pointed to three seats in the audience marked RESERVED. "The other panel members will be in the front row for this segment. They'll come on stage after the formal presentation."

"That's when I press the red button."

Mike clapped me on the back. "The kid's a genius."

Jeanne shook her head. "Don't flatter him. He'll want to give the lecture." She turned to me. "Well, genius, we'd better get out to the lobby."

A small table and two chairs were positioned in front of the main entrance to the lecture hall. Jeanne and I each had a sign-in sheet so we could register attendees as quickly as possible. Most of them were from the Southeast, mainly from the major universities and medical complexes. I noticed a few media representatives—*New England Journal of Medicine*, *Discovery Magazine*, and *Scientific American*.

"How's it going?" The voice came from behind us.

I swiveled around to see a tall man lean over Jeanne and study her sheet.

"Pretty well," she answered. "You about ready to start?"

"We'll wait a few minutes." He looked at me and offered his hand. "I'm John Everston."

Before I could speak, Jeanne said, "I'm sorry. This is Gene Adamson. Gene, this is my father."

I started to get up, but he patted me on the shoulder. "Gene. Of course. Good to finally meet you. My Jeanne talks about you all the time."

"Really?" I sputtered, then mentally kicked myself for sounding like a dork.

"Yes, really. Thanks for helping out today." And he was gone, disappearing through the doors.

"You want to go on in?" Jeanne asked. "I can handle the stragglers."

The lecturer, Dr. Colbert, was a short, frizzy-haired man in his sixties who could barely see over the podium. He spoke for about ten minutes, maybe a minute of which I understood. Most of his talk was laced with references to enzymes and their gene-splitting actions. I tuned my ears for one sentence: "May I have the first slide, please."

The cue came and I pressed the green button flawlessly. Four years at Harvard could not have improved my performance. The lights dimmed, and I struggled against sleep as my six A.M. wakeup began to exact its price. Twice, I almost pushed the red button, thinking the lecture was over. But Dr. Colbert had only paused to allow his audience time to study whatever was on the screen. I couldn't see anything but the glare of the projection beam.

I tried standing on one foot to keep myself alert. Then I began rolling a quarter across my fingers, an exercise that keeps a magician's hands nimble. Fifteen minutes into the slides and five minutes into my mind-less quarter manipulation, I saw movement directly across the stage. At first, I thought my sleepy eyes were playing tricks on me. The opposite wing was mostly lost in shadows, but then the shape appeared again, faintly illuminated by the spill light from the screen. A man crouched beside the extra chair. I could see a glint off his glasses as he shifted his position. He rested his hand upon the chair arm and a second glint flared.

The quarter tumbled from my fingers and rolled across the stage. The sight of the pistol jolted me wide awake.

5

I froze. Dr. Colbert's monologue drowned out the clink of the wayward coin. My backstage corner must have been so dark the gunman hadn't noticed me. His attention seemed riveted on the back of the speaker. What was he planning? He could have shot Colbert ten times by now. I wanted to run for a security guard, find anyone better equipped to deal with a potential killer. But what if he acted while I was gone?

The words erupted, driven out of me by overwhelming fear. "Gun! There's a man with a gun!" I slammed my hand against the red button.

The gunman turned and lunged in my direction. Dr. Colbert halted with a confused stammer. He saw the other man dart behind the screen. Colbert threw his hands up, protecting his face. The gunman only glanced at him, then looked back at me, probably to see if I were armed.

The audience watched the scene unfold as the screen rose and the projector beam spread over the stage. Shouts grew louder and more frantic. "Gun! Get down! He's got a gun!"

The man strained against the blinding light, searching the front row. He rushed forward and fired three shots. Their roar exploded like a cannon in the small auditorium. House lights blazed to life. People jammed the aisles, desperate to escape. Two security guards were on the far side, their guns drawn, trying to get a clear shot.

The man brandished the pistol above his head. "God's will be done! God is eternal for the eternal!" He must have seen the approaching guards for instead of retreating the way he came, he ran toward me. I shrank back as he brushed past me, only to stop at the solid wall. There was no exit on this side. Before I could bolt to safety, the man grabbed my arm with his left hand and wrenched it behind my back. The pistol barrel pressed against my throat, burning my skin with its hot muzzle.

"Stay back!" he yelled to the guards. "Stay back and no one else gets hurt!"

The two security men had climbed onto the stage, but came no closer. The noise in the lecture hall abruptly ceased as everyone stared at the gunman and his hostage. Everyone except Jeanne. She bent over the body of her father, sobbing out his name, "John, John."

One of the guards spoke as calmly as he could. "No one is going to get hurt. Let the boy go and lay the gun on the floor."

"No!" The man twisted my arm even tighter. "He'll be released when I'm outside. Clear that exit!" He snapped his head to signal he wanted them offstage. The guard nodded to his partner and they backed up a few steps, vacating the way to the back-stage exit.

I recognized the second guard. Billy McKay. He'd stopped by the playroom a few times when I was entertaining the children. I'd showed him how to do a few magic tricks for his own kids.

"Don't worry, Adamson," he said. "We won't let you drop out of sight."

I made the connection as the man pushed me toward the door. I just needed the opportunity.

Jeanne looked up from her father. "No," she screamed. "He'll kill you, Gene. He'll kill all of us."

The man looked from the guards to the girl kneeling below him. I felt his grip relax slightly and he moved the gun off my neck and pointed it at Jeanne. Drop out of sight, I thought. One of the tricks I had taught the guard in which a small ball drops out of his hand into a hidden pouch. I kicked my legs out from under me. Gravity yanked my hundred-and-fifty-pound body faster than any other movement I could make. My arm unwound behind me, stabbing with pain, but I fell to the floor, leaving my captor exposed.

Again, three shots crashed through the lecture hall. Two from the guards hit the man in the chest, knocking him backwards. His own bullet splintered the ceiling.

My ears still rang from the explosions as I rolled free. I slapped the gun from the man's hand. His breath gurgled and his eyes went in and out of focus on my face. He tried to speak. I should have scrambled away, but I was drawn closer.

He coughed one word. "Gene." He managed to draw a deeper breath. "Gene Adamson."

Unbelievably, he'd pieced my name together from what he'd heard the guard and Jeanne say. He repeated it, but now the whisper was barely audible. I put my ear to his lips.

"The list. You're on the list. God's chosen Gene."

My name came in a release of air. No other breath followed.

I started crying. I felt like a fool, but the pent-up tension burst out of me in tears.

The guard, Billy McKay, put his arm around me. "You all right?"

I could only nod my head.

"You got the trick just right. You're one heck of a magician, kid. You never lost your nerve."

I never lost my nerve? There I sat bawling like a baby. Jeanne had lost her father. I wanted my mother.

6

"Dad, I'm all right." I twisted the phone cord in my hand and leaned over the mahogany desk as if that would emphasize my words.

"I'm flying home." Dad's voice was low and tense. The administrative assistant of some bank president in Chicago had interrupted their negotiations so my father could take my call.

"No, really, I'm fine. It was just scary for a few minutes." I knew there was nothing he could do. My dad worked in Mergers and Acquisitions for Bank of America and the Chicago meeting was a critical step in folding a mid-sized, mid-western institution into the mega-bank. B O G, I called it—Bank of the Galaxy. "Dad, I wouldn't have bothered you except I'm afraid it's going to be on the news. Maybe even in Chicago. The guy was a nut and I was in the wrong place at the wrong time."

"Are you sure? Everyone here understands if I have to leave. Sometimes these things hit you harder later."

"I'll be okay. I'll feel worse if you think I'm too young to handle it. Dr. Lockaby told me to take a few days off with pay. He's offered to let me talk to a counselor if I want to."

"A counselor? He says you need a counselor?"

"No. He just made the offer. He's been very helpful. I'm calling from his office. It makes yours look like a closet."

I heard my father chuckle. He probably thought I was exaggerating, but Dr. Paul Lockaby was President and CEO of Carolinas Medical Center and all its satellite hospitals in the region. The office could have held a small army.

"Okay," Dad agreed, "but promise me you'll check in every evening and morning. You've got the number of my hotel."

"I promise. There's one other thing," and I moved on to the primary reason I interrupted his meeting. "A detective wants to speak with you."

"Me? About what?"

"He needs to ask me some questions about what happened."

"I thought you were just in the wrong place at the wrong time." The urgency again rose in his voice.

"It's Dr. Lockaby's idea. Since I'm under eighteen, he wants to make sure you approve. A formality."

"A statement for the police report I guess. Okay, put him on."

"Just a second." I laid down the receiver. The phone buttons looked too complicated for me to place him on hold. I walked across the thick carpet to the office door. Lockaby had given me privacy once the call went through. He and Detective Carl Drakesford waited in the adjoining office of the executive secretary.

"My dad's ready to talk to you."

"Come on then," the detective replied. "You too, Dr. Lockaby. You qualify as a witness."

Drakesford worked out of the Homicide Division of the Charlotte Police Department. He didn't look like a cop. He looked like basketball star Michael Jordan at fifty. He must have stood six-foot-five, his head was smoothly shaved, and he flashed a Michael Jordan smile that made you want to like him and buy whatever he was selling.

Dr. Lockaby waved me into a guest chair beside him as Drakesford sat behind the CEO's desk and picked up the phone.

"Mr. Adamson, I'm Carl Drakesford, Charlotte police. You've got quite a boy, sir."

There was a long pause during which I hoped my father was agreeing with him.

"That's what he said? Wrong place at the wrong time?" Drakesford winked at me. "Well, that's not exactly what I've heard from some other witnesses. They say your son was at the right place at the right time. His actions probably saved lives. He certainly saved the life of Dr. Everston's daughter."

The moment crystallized in my mind. I saw the pistol move from my neck and point at Jeanne. That was when I fell. Perhaps I had saved her life.

"I'd like your permission to get a statement from Gene. He won't have to come to the station. We can do it here. You're welcome to listen in." There was another pause. Detective Drakesford pulled a pen and small notepad out of his inside suit pocket. The smart tailoring of his clothes was a long way from a TV detective's crummy raincoat. Drakesford jotted down something, then read a string of numbers into the phone. "Good. I'll see that a copy is faxed to your hotel. Do you have anything else to say to Gene?"

Drakesford held the phone across the desk.

"Dad?"

"Since when did you go humble on me?"

"I hadn't really thought about it that way."

"I'm proud of you, son. And your mother would be, too." His voice broke.

A lump lodged in my throat. "Thanks," was all I could say. I hung up and sat down.

Drakesford put a pocket-size tape recorder on the desk between us. "Pull your chair closer." He flipped to a clean page in his pad and gave me that Michael Jordan grin. "Nothing to be nervous about. I'll make some notes and use the tape to extract more detail as I need it. I'll fax your dad a copy to review before you sign it. Fair enough?"

I looked to Dr. Lockaby for reassurance.

"Sounds fine to me, Gene."

"Okay," I said.

Drakesford looked at his watch and clicked on the machine. "This is Detective Carl Drakesford with Dr. Paul Lockaby and Gene Adamson. It's two-thirty on the afternoon of July sixth and we're in Dr. Lockaby's office at Carolinas Medical Center."

Two-thirty, I thought. A little over two hours ago, I had a pistol at my throat. It seemed like a year ago.

Drakesford asked me to begin with how I happened to be in the lecture hall. When I got to the part where I first spotted the man crouching by the chair, he interrupted. "We have a tentative I.D. Vermont driver's license issued to Sidney Chamberlain. I'm told the photo matches. Ever heard of him?"

"No. And I never saw him before in my life."

"Well, we're trying to find a next of kin. The crime lab's going through the lecture hall, then they'll lift prints off the body here in the hospital morgue. Maybe he's got a record. So you saw him by the chair, holding the pistol."

I continued through the part where the guard Billy McKay led me off the stage and into a nearby private office. Then I asked Drakesford a question. "Did this Sidney Chamberlain say anything more?"

"No. The room was full of doctors. They tried to assist both him and Everston. Emergency room personnel arrived almost immediately, but I think that final breath, when he said your name, was his last. The list. You're on the list. Do you have any idea what list he was talking about?"

"No. I wish I did. He must have been delusional calling me God's chosen. Maybe he knows another Gene Adamson. He heard my name, he was shot, dying, and thought he was seeing someone else."

Drakesford clicked off the tape recorder.

Dr. Lockaby cleared his throat. "I think we'll find he's mentally deranged. Why else would he murder an innocent doctor who's trying to help couples have babies?"

"You may want to beef up your internal security,"

Drakesford suggested. "I'll request some extra passes by our patrol cruisers for the next couple of days. Is the hospital's public information department dealing with the press?"

"Yes," Dr. Lockaby said. "We brought everybody in to handle the media. Not only local but CNN and the major wire services. We've told them Dr. Everston and an unknown gunman were both killed. Other questions are being referred to the police."

"I'll brief our people." Drakesford turned his attention to me. "Gene, you'll have to deal with the press—"

The phone intercom cut him off. "Dr. Lockaby?"

Lockaby clenched the arm of his chair. "I told you I can't be disturbed."

"I know," replied the nameless woman without any trace of fear. "It's for the detective. One of his officers demands to speak to him. He's on line five."

Drakesford's eyebrows arched in surprise. He punched a flashing button and put the receiver to his ear. "Drakesford."

The expression on his face hardened from curiosity to utmost concentration. Michael Jordan was at the foul line with the game on the line. He spoke through gritted teeth. "Say nothing. I'll have Dr. Lockaby bring me to you." He set the receiver down gently and swept his gaze across both of us. "Well, you should have tightened security already, Dr. Lockaby. Sidney Chamberlain's body is missing."

"That's preposterous. It must be a filing error. Rare, but it happens, especially if the morgue is busy. Maybe they mixed him up with Dr. Everston."

Drakesford's eyes narrowed. "That's the interesting part. Dr. Everston's body is also gone. The killer and his victim have disappeared."

7

Dr. Lockaby was speechless. He gasped for air like a goldfish who'd jumped out of his bowl.

Drakesford's smile was back, but his dark eyes kept their competitive intensity. "Well, Gene, looks like our theory of a lone gunman just got flushed down the john. I need you on my team for awhile."

Michael Jordan asking me to be on his team. "Sure."

Drakesford turned to Dr. Lockaby. "Can you keep Gene here in the hospital for a few days? For free? I don't want his father having to file a bogus insurance claim to pay the bill."

"Yes, but why?"

Drakesford looked at me. "Gene, before that call came through, I was going to warn you that the press is perched outside ready to pounce on you. You're news, you're the hostage. They'll want you to relive every second, describe every feeling, and they'll press you to make your account as dramatic as possible, regardless of whether it's true or not."

"I don't have to talk to them, do I?"

"No, but I'm afraid in this country, freedom of the press is easier to guarantee than freedom from the press. I don't want you in an awkward position, having to face the cameras and reporters without your father, especially if these bodies have been taken."

"You think he's in danger?" Lockaby asked.

"I didn't say that," Drakesford snapped. "If someone's got wind of your problem in the morgue, Gene might be asked about it. If your PR people say he's staying in the hospital for routine observation, we can keep Gene isolated a little longer. Right now, we don't know squat about who, how, or why. I'm not proud. I'm requesting the FBI. This smells of some extensive organization to have been cleaned up so quickly."

I only half heard Drakesford's words. I was still distracted by Lockaby's question: "You think he's in danger?"

"What about Jeanne Everston?" I asked Drakesford.

"What about her?"

"Some extensive organization sounds like you're afraid to say conspiracy. This Chamberlain was trying to kill Jeanne."

"I've got an officer talking to her. We'll make sure she's protected."

Dr. Lockaby and Detective Drakesford left for the morgue. I waited in the office for arrangements to be made for my room. I'd have to call Dad and explain why I wasn't at home. He'd definitely want to fly back now and that was fine with me. Bodies just don't get up and walk away. Or, if they did, I hoped they weren't carrying a list that included my name.

After nearly half an hour, the door opened and a pretty brunette walked in. She must have been about ten years older than me but close and cute enough that I didn't want to come across as a scared kid.

"I'm Rachel Denning, Assistant for Media Affairs. I'll be your contact while you're here."

I stood up.

She seemed surprised I matched her height. "Dr. Lockaby assigned you to the Children's Hospital?"

"That's what I requested. I work there."

"Oh, right. I knew that. I'm usually not so scattered. It's been quite a day."

"You're telling me."

"Right again. Nobody knows better than you."

Except for Jeanne Everston. I wondered if she had relatives coming in. She'd told me her mother was dead. That was something we had in common. I also wondered if the hospital had told her about the disappearance of her father's body.

"Do you think that will be all right?" Rachel Denning asked.

I didn't know what "that" she was talking about. My mind had shut her out. "Sorry. Say again?"

"For me to be with you when you check out. Not that you're officially checked in. To help with the press. Get their questions over all at once."

"I guess so. Let me talk to my dad first."

"Certainly." She led me past the empty desk of Dr. Lockaby's secretary and out a side door. "There were a half-dozen reporters camped at the elevators. We'll go up the back stairs and walk over to the children's wing."

The hospital was a sprawling complex and Rachel Denning took me on a circuitous route which would have required my dropping bread crumbs if I were to find my way back. At last, we emerged from a stairwell at the end of one of the children's hallways. Miss Denning hustled me into the closest room.

"Gene! Thank God!" Nurse Helen McBride smothered me in a hug. "We've been so worried."

I squirmed free. "I'm okay. Just a little dazed."

"I was off at three, but I couldn't leave till I knew for sure you were safe. Right, Janet?"

She turned to a woman behind her. Mrs. Janet Malkovski stepped forward and gave me a more restrained hug. She wasn't a nurse but served as coordinator of the hospital's organ donor program. Mom, Dad, and I met with her when there was a possibility Mom could receive a liver transplant. Dad and I had our tissue typed in case the doctors thought even a partial transplant could help, but Mom's condition deteriorated too rapidly and a compatible organ wasn't found in time. Mrs. Malkovski had stayed in touch through the whole ordeal. She managed to nurture hope without being phony and to help our family cope when hope was gone.

Mrs. Malkovski stepped back and looked me up and down. "I was with Mr. and Mrs. Thompson when Helen said you were being assigned this room. Not in your name. Toby Doggett."

Odd choice but I guessed less obvious than John Doe.

"Where's your father?" Mrs. Malkovski asked.

"In Chicago. I called him."

"Oh, my," Nurse McBride said. "You're here alone. Do you need me to bring you anything?"

I thought about clean underwear, pajamas, a toothbrush, and a good mystery to take my mind off the one I was living. I thought about the messy state of my room and how Nurse McBride would need to rummage through my drawers. "It's probably just for the night. Maybe you could get them to smuggle me some ice cream with dinner."

"You're getting a steak," Rachel Denning said. "I put you on the list as a new father."

The PR department was buying my cooperation with food. A fair exchange. Maybe that was the list Chamberlain meant. Somehow I doubted a steak was the big reward for "God's chosen."

"Good," Nurse McBride agreed, "and I'll leave a note for the night shift not to poke and prod you."

The three women started for the door.

"Mrs. Malkovski, could I talk to you a minute?" When the other two had left, I closed the door. "You said you were talking to Katherine Thompson's parents. Any news?"

"She's resting comfortably. She had a good bit of fluid drained and she may be able to go home for a couple weeks."

"As long as she stays ready."

Mrs. Malkovski shook her head. "She needs a break, Gene. A lucky break."

A lucky break. If the call came, the Thompsons would have fifteen minutes to respond or the next name on the list would be paged. Katherine had to be at the hospital in under an hour. I couldn't imagine the pressure of waiting, the fear that the call wouldn't come, the fear and joy if it did, and the joy and grief—joy that Katherine could be saved, the grief of another mother and father whose own child had perished.

"I thought maybe today would be the day," Mrs. Malkovski said. "My counterpart at Duke University Hospital told me a nine-year-old boy suffered brain damage from a car wreck. His parents consented to donate. Evidently, someone else ranked higher because the National Organ Procurement Center never called. Little Katherine has got to be in the top tier. Her condition is growing critical, and she's been listed since December. The normal wait is sixty to seventy days. Katherine's over a hundred and eighty."

"How often do they update her condition?"

"Her doctor makes the assessment. He's had her coded top priority for over two months. It's tough. There just aren't enough donors."

"It's tough because more people have to die."

Mrs. Malkovski rested her hand on my arm. "The deaths will come and they are tragic, but the double tragedy is how other children will die when useful, vital organs are embalmed, buried, and denied to those who desperately need them."

"I'm probably the only kid in high school who has a living will. Dad and I are both donors."

I could see from her face we shared the same thought: I had come too close to being harvested.

"And just stay that way," she said. "A potential donor." She grabbed her purse off the bed. "I've got to run. You stay put. I saw a reporter from the paper out at the nurses' station."

"So I'm Toby Doggett."

Mrs. Malkovski laughed. "Dr. Lockaby's personal choice, no doubt. Toby's the name of his miniature schnauzer."

"So much for my hero status."

"If your ego needs a boost, talk to Katherine Thompson. One of the orderlies made the mistake of mentioning the shooting while Katherine was being wheeled back to her room. She became hysterical. Who's Goober?"

"A song I taught her," I said, not wanting to have yet another person tag me with the nickname.

"A song, huh? Well, when you're no longer in hiding, go see her. She'll be thrilled."

Mrs. Malkovski closed the door, leaving me alone in a room with painted animal faces grinning from the walls. The television remote hanging by the bedside was bright orange with oversized purple buttons. I thought about slipping off my Nikes, lying down, and pressing the channel selector until "Gilligan's Island" inevitably came on the screen.

What I really wanted to do was talk to Jeanne, tell her how sorry I was, see if there was anything I could do, let her know I was cooperating with a police investigation and not ignoring her. Several months ago, I'd committed her number to memory. The phone sat just beyond the orange and purple remote.

Eerie and chilling to hear her father's voice sound so alive on the answering machine. "You've reached the Everstons. Neither Jeanne nor I are available. Please leave a brief message and we'll return your call as soon as possible. Thank you."

I faltered for a few seconds, uncertain how to
begin, yet afraid if I didn't say something, the machine
would cut off. "Jeanne, it's Gene. I'm still at the
hospital. The police have asked me to stay here, away
from the press. They think there might be a conspiracy, but they've probably told you that. I'm so
sorry for you. If there's anything I or my dad can do,
please call. I'm in room 718, but under the name of
Toby. Toby Doggett. Bye for now."

I hung up, surprised that my heart started racing.
It wasn't because of Jeanne, but because a sense of
danger unexpectedly surged inside me. Should I have
left so much information? My room number? My code
name? What if someone other than Jeanne checked
the machine? Well, I couldn't undo what was now on
her tape. At least she'd know I cared.

I also cared about Katherine Thompson. She lay a
few rooms up the hall, worrying about me while her
own plight grew worse. If seeing me would give her
some comfort, there was nothing more important I
could do.

I listened at my door. Quiet. I heard only a
blending of different television programs coming from
other rooms. The staff wouldn't be bringing the dinner
carts up until five. Another half hour. I cracked the
door and looked down the hall. At the far end, one of
the nurses stood with her back to me while making
notes on a chart. Her body blocked my view of the
station, but it also obstructed anyone else's view of
me. Katherine was four doors down on the other side.
Her door was partially closed and the interior dark.

She was probably sleeping after her ordeal of the morning.

I walked briskly along the hall so that the nurse continued to shield me. When I was directly opposite 711, I darted into her room.

She was alone, lying on the bed with her head turned three-quarters away and facing the shaded window. A chair sat by the bedside with a folded newspaper in its seat. The crossword puzzle was half-finished. Her mom or dad must have gone out for a few minutes. I put the newspaper on the credenza and eased into the chair.

Katherine's breathing was shallow. Her skin seemed almost translucent and the light blue veins of her forehead rose up like rounded ridges. There was a light film of perspiration on her face. Her colorless lips puckered in and out and her eyes squinted shut with irregular contractions. The frail hands clutched the favorite, frayed teddy bear to her chest. She was restless, caught in the prison of some bad dream.

The sight was so familiar. Many an hour I sat by my mother's hospital bed, watching her fitful sleep, sadly aware that the calm, comforting demeanor she projected for Dad and me must have been stripped away by the fear in her subconscious.

I don't know how long I had been humming. I was just aware that my own subconscious had responded and the melody of "Goober Peas" softly vibrated in my throat. I began to whisper the words:

"Sittin' by the roadside on a summer's day,
Chattin' with my messmates, passing time away,
Lying in the shadow, underneath the trees,

Goodness, how delicious, eating goober peas!
Peas! Peas! Peas! Peas! . . ."

It was then I heard her faint voice join me. "Eating goober peas! Goodness, how delicious, eating goober peas!"

She rolled over and smiled. "You're here? You're all right?"

"Well, you're here and you're all right. Why shouldn't I be?"

Her lips trembled and tears flowed from the large brown eyes. "They said someone tried to shoot you."

"I disappeared right in front of him. You know what a trickster I am." I pulled two tissues from the box on the credenza and dabbed her cheeks. "Now stop crying or the nurses will think you're in pain and give you a shot. Then you will have something to cry about."

"I'm not in pain. It's my dream. I'm crying about my dream."

"What dream?"

"The one I just had. We were home and the call came. My new heart was on its way. I had to get to the hospital. Mommy and Daddy were going crazy. They couldn't find the suitcases, they couldn't find the car keys, and they couldn't remember how to drive here. I kept asking for you. I knew you would calm them down. You'd get me to my new heart. But I couldn't find you and I was scared. Mommy and Daddy said you were dead. I was crying. I was going to die, too. Then I heard the song. I heard you singing the song. You were coming. I knew you were coming. I opened my eyes and here you are."

I patted her hand. "Here I am."

She grabbed my wrist with a strength that surprised me. "Promise you'll be here for real. When it's time for real. Please, Gene? Promise?" She sniffled, and the tears started again.

"I promise," I said and hoped my own tears didn't show.

THE PRESENT

8

I've looked back over my words, and I realize the events of that day—the murder, the disappearance of the bodies, little Katherine's dream—all are critical to report because they chart the course of my story. However, even now I'm vain enough to worry that I sound like a nerd, a boy who pines away for his dead mother, a boy who has no life other than to sigh over a beautiful classmate, a boy who lives in isolation with his music and magic because he has no social skills.

Well, how glamorous is high school anyway? Most of it's routine. We can have friends we hang with and not have a special girlfriend or boyfriend. I had my own crowd of regulars and we'd go to football games and weekend parties. It's just that I wasn't at the top of the social chain. Maybe if there was a category for "Most Likely to Continue Life as an Ordinary Guy," I would have won.

I remember wondering what my friends were making of my name being spread all over the news. Would Kevin Ferris give some stupid quote like "I was surprised Goober could think fast enough." Yes, my image was as important to me as to any teenager. So you'll understand that after visiting Katherine and making my promise, . . .

THE PAST

9

. . . I began to worry what was being said about me. Would the TV news use the dopey picture from hospital personnel?

Katherine's parents returned a few minutes before five. I was touched by their genuine concern and assured them I was okay. I also asked them not to tell anyone I was in the Children's Hospital.

I excused myself when I heard the rattle of the dinner carts in the hall. Although I didn't expect the promised steak dinner to arrive with the Monday night chicken the rest of the floor was eating, I certainly didn't want my meal going back to the kitchen because I wasn't there.

A phone rang. The sound grew louder as I neared my room. I ran the last few yards and grabbed the receiver just in time to hear a click and a dial tone. Perhaps it was only Rachel Denning asking how I wanted my steak. I wanted it now. I hadn't eaten since breakfast. In my heart, I feared the call had been from Jeanne. I punched her number and heard her father's voice begin again. I hung up.

The five-thirty newscast led with the shooting. A stern-faced woman reporter stood outside the emergency room door and spoke in hushed tones of the "crazed assassin" and the tragic, senseless loss of Dr. John Everston. Then there was pre-recorded footage of the lecture hall, now webbed in police tape with crime lab technicians dutifully searching for clues. The station cut back to the reporter who introduced Rachel Denning of the Carolinas Medical Center's Department of Public Information. Rachel stepped into the shot and moistened her lips. Seeing her nervous glance at the camera, I was glad Detective Drakesford had protected me from such a hot seat.

"We understand the gunman held a hostage for a few minutes," the reporter said. "A high school student—Eugene Adamson—"

The television flashed up my hospital personnel photograph in all its magnificent splendor. The only thing I needed was the word "GOOBER" under it to make my humiliation complete.

"—and he's been admitted to the hospital?"

Rachel Denning nodded. "Gene Adamson is here for observation. He wasn't physically injured, but as the gunman attempted to forcibly take him from the lecture hall, young Adamson fainted—"

Fainted! Fainted! How could she say that? Detective Drakesford called me a hero. Dr. Lockaby agreed. The guard Billy McKay congratulated me.

"—and everyone wants to make sure he's completely recovered."

My reputation had just been hijacked by a story

created to explain my presence in the hospital. What did they care if I spent my senior year as "Sir Goober the Chicken-Hearted?"

"Is Mr. Doggett here?"

I turned from the TV to see a young Hispanic woman in the doorway. I clicked off the set before the treacherous Miss Denning announced I'd been so scared I'd peed in my pants.

"Mr. Doggett?" I asked without thinking.

"Toby Doggett." She checked a card in her hand. "I have his steak dinner. Room seven-eighteen."

"Oh, Doggett. He's in the bathroom." I nodded to the closed door. "I'm his uh, nephew. Uncle Dog, we call him. You can leave it with me." I stopped babbling before I said something really stupid. Fortunately, my picture hadn't been on the screen when she came in, not that she would have recognized me.

She pulled a cart in behind her. Nice gold-trimmed bone china, "CMC" engraved silverware, and a white linen napkin completed the place setting for a mammoth sirloin, baked potato, and asparagus tips. My appetite, which had shriveled into oblivion at Rachel Denning's comments, bounced back with a vengeance.

After I had eaten everything but the floral pattern on the plate, I tried to reach Dad at his Chicago hotel. The hotel operator said his room was guaranteed on his credit card, but he had yet to check in. She transferred me into his assigned voicemail and I gave my Doggett room number and the reason I was staying at the hospital. The receiver had barely touched the cradle when the phone rang.

"Toby Doggett's room."

"I tried to call you back, but there was no answer."

"Jeanne," I said, recognizing her voice immediately. "Jeanne, I'm so sorry."

"Thank you. I'd rather not talk about it over the phone." She spoke in flat, mechanical syllables. "I didn't realize you were hurt."

"I'm not. The police want to keep me away from the press." I started to say until they find your father's body, but I didn't know what Drakesford's people had told her. "Have you talked to the police?"

"No, I'm fine. Did you get your guitar?"

This conversation was very strange. I wondered if she was in shock.

"I guess it's still in the playroom where I left it this morning."

"Funny, with all that's happened, I thought about it. I'd feel better if you had it with you. Promise me you'll get it now."

"All right. Is there anything else I can do for you?"

"Be careful," she said and hung up.

Was the poor girl alone and overwhelmed by all that had happened? She didn't sound like the same person I sat beside in history class, the same person I met in the parking lot this morning. My guitar? Why would she worry about my guitar? Grief does strange things to people.

I remembered the week after we buried my mother, my father had to hand wax both our cars. He obsessed with getting them in immaculate condition and spent a full day detailing each. In another week, they were as dirty as ever and he didn't care.

I buzzed the nurses' station and asked if any reporters were hanging out.

"No," the duty nurse replied. "Can I bring you something?"

"I'd like to walk a little. I stuffed myself with dinner."

She laughed and said she'd have someone from dining remove the tray. "And the coast is clear if you want to jog through the halls."

It was nearly seven, quiet time on the children's floor. The Child Life staff had picked up the playroom in anticipation of a new day. The colored building blocks were neatly stacked in a corner, picture books were displayed on toddler-high shelves, assorted balls, games, and puzzles lay packed away in toy chests. The only light came from the glow of the aquarium built into the wall between the room and hallway. I peered through the angel fish and saw no one on the other side. The hum of the air pump and gurgle of aquarium bubbles masked the sound of my footsteps as I slipped into the room and closed the door behind me.

I'd left my guitar in the closet where we kept art supplies and the triangles, drums, and other percussion instruments for the kids' rhythm band. I reached in and grabbed the handle of my guitar case. The stiff edge of construction paper scraped the back of my hand.

I pulled loose a note that had been wedged under the lip of the case and walked closer to the pool of light cast by the aquarium. "Wait here by phone,

Wallingford" was printed in black ink in the center of the green paper. Jeanne had left a message in the name of our history teacher. She'd been up on this floor but had not come to see me. Maybe she'd even called from the playroom.

The telephone rang. I nearly jumped out of my skin.

"Hello," I whispered.

"Are you alone?"

"Yes. Jeanne, what's going on?"

"What did Chamberlain say to you?"

"Chamberlain?"

"That man who shot . . ." She hesitated a second. ". . . who shot my father."

"He didn't say anything that made any sense. The list. He said I was on some kind of list. That I was God's chosen."

"What did he say exactly? It's very important."

I heard the dying man's whisper again in my ear. "He said, 'The list. You're on the list. God's chosen Gene.'"

"Who else have you told this to?"

"The police. A Detective Drakesford. And Dr. Lockaby."

"Where were you when I first tried to call you? After you left me the message."

"I went down the hall to visit little Katherine Thompson. She's the girl I told you is waiting on a heart transplant."

"Did you mention any of this to her or her parents?"

"No. Look, Jeanne, what's the matter?"

"You and I are in danger. And anyone we talk to. You're sure you didn't say anything?"

"Katherine was worried about me. She'd heard about the shooting and I'm worried about her. She got passed over again and her condition is getting desperate."

"Passed over?"

"A potential donor. Somebody jumped ahead of her on the list."

The list. The word exploded in my head. Why hadn't I thought of it before? "Jeanne, do you think that could be it? The list of patients waiting for transplants?"

She didn't answer, but I could hear the sound of her breathing.

"Or the list of donors," I added. "I'm on that list. My tissue was typed for my mother."

"Gene, you've got to be very careful. There are people in high places who could be making money. A lot of money. You can't trust Dr. Lockaby. You can't trust the police. They may be keeping you in the hospital to control who you talk to. The phone in your room might be bugged."

"Why do you think that?"

"My father is dead!" she shouted into the phone. "What more proof do I need? We can only trust each other. Everyone, and I mean everyone, could be the next person to pull the trigger."

The door opened and the lights came on. Detective Carl Drakesford stared at me. He wasn't smiling.

10

For a few seconds, the breath caught in my throat. My brain raced for an answer to his unasked question: what was I doing here?

"Detective Drakesford, you startled me." I heard Jeanne hang up instantly. "Excuse me." I pressed zero, then replaced the receiver. "Voicemail. Checking messages at home."

"Something wrong with the phone in your room?" Drakesford walked in, followed by a young man with short-clipped black hair and wearing a dark blue suit that perfectly matched Drakesford's. He must have been half a foot shorter than the detective, nearer my five-nine height.

"No. I came to get my guitar. I work in this room."

"You always make phone calls in the dark?" the second man asked. There was neither warmth in his voice nor humor in his eyes.

"The nurses are trying to get the children settled for the night. Turning on the light is an invitation to come into the playroom." I looked at Drakesford. "I'm sorry. I thought I was a guest here. I didn't realize I was confined to my room."

Drakesford ignored my sarcasm. He nodded to his companion who came over, picked up the telephone. Caller I.D., I thought. They would check the last connection and know I was lying.

Drakesford looked around the room. "We need to talk, Gene. Here's as good a place as any." He closed the door and turned out the lights. "Have a seat."

I sat on a floor cushion in the shadows beyond the dim reach of the aquarium's bulb. Drakesford crouched down like a quarterback forming a huddle. He studied the backs of his massive hands for a minute, waiting for his partner to finish.

The man on the telephone grunted. "364-8871."

I was glad the darkness concealed my face because I felt like someone had just punched me in the stomach. The man had recited my home phone number.

"Okay, Gene, who was on your answering machine?" the man asked.

"Wait a minute," I said, mustering as much indignation as I could. "I may not be an adult, but I know my rights. Get Dr. Lockaby in here. He wouldn't even let you take my statement without first talking to my father. Maybe I do want to speak to the press."

"Now calm down," Drakesford said. "Let's start over. I'm afraid we've jumped to conclusions ourselves. I apologize. Gene, this is Agent Jason Lambert of the FBI. He specializes in cults and he's investigating Dr. Everston's murder for the Bureau. We're working together."

With the introduction, I stood up and stepped into the pool of light. "Good to meet you." I shook his hand firmly.

Drakesford rose to tower above both of us. "Let's go back to your room. We've just got a few questions. Won't take but a minute."

I thought I knew who those few questions were about and decided I'd sound more innocent asking questions rather than answering them. The telephone trace could mean only one thing: Jeanne Everston was hiding in my house.

"What's happened to Dr. Everston's daughter?" I asked.

Drakesford shrugged. "What makes you think something's happened to her?"

"I've tried to reach her at home. No answer. Not even a relative. I don't understand why no one's there. You said you were going to warn her. Do you know where she is?" I didn't have to fake the concern. I was scared for her and for me.

A glance passed between the two law officers. When the bodies disappeared, Drakesford said he'd be bringing in the FBI. Now that Lambert was here, I wondered who was in charge.

"Gene, we couldn't find her," Drakesford admitted. "We hoped maybe you'd talked to her."

"I told you she was in danger."

"Look," Lambert said. "There's no reason to believe anything's happened to her. She's frightened. She's probably hiding."

"With good reason. Have you found her father's body?"

Lambert ignored the question. "You need to let us know if she contacts you." He slipped his hand in the pocket of his pressed suit coat and withdrew a business card. I saw the FBI crest and a ten-digit number. "You can reach me from anywhere in the world, anytime. Call me immediately if you hear from her."

"No." For the first time, I saw the hard, cool, professional demeanor of both men crack. My obstinate refusal surprised them.

"This is a criminal investigation," Drakesford said sharply.

"Yes, but Jeanne and I aren't the criminals. So stop treating us like we were."

"Jeanne Everston might be," Agent Lambert said.

"What?" I heard my voice ask the question, but my mind lurched forward in confusion. Jeanne, my seventeen-year-old classmate, the girl I thought about constantly, a criminal, hunted by the FBI? If Lambert meant to unnerve me, he certainly succeeded.

"Be careful," Drakesford said. The warning was for Lambert, not me.

"I am being careful," Lambert snapped. "I don't want a case of puppy love to screw up the investigation."

Puppy love? His insult to my age and my feelings was more than I could take, but I didn't know what to do. I wanted to storm off, slamming doors behind me. They'd say I was acting like a teenager. I had to know what Lambert meant and I bit my tongue and waited.

"Jeanne Everston has been seen only once since her father was killed," Lambert said. "The attendant in the morgue said she came down to collect her father's personal property."

"When?"

"About one. An hour and a half after the shooting. The police investigators hadn't examined the bodies yet. Because the shooting occurred in a hospital, the victims were immediately taken to the emergency room. Attempts were made at resuscitation. Then, when they were pronounced dead, their bodies went into the system and standard police procedures were delayed."

"Jeanne had a right to her father's belongings," I said.

"Yes," Lambert agreed. "But it wasn't her father's belongings she claimed. She insisted there had been a mix-up. She said her father had a computer disk in his pocket. She made the attendant retrieve the personal effects of Chamberlain, the shooter. A CD-ROM in a yellow sleeve was one of the items."

"Then how do you know there wasn't a mix-up?" I asked, desperate to defend Jeanne's innocence.

"Because an orderly came in with an empty gurney while they were talking. No one else was on duty. The attendant told the man he'd be with him in a moment and turned his attention to Jeanne. He vaguely remembers the orderly moving behind him, and then a soaked rag was pressed tightly over his nose and mouth. Ether. When he regained consciousness, Jeanne, the orderly, the gurney, the personal property of both Dr. Everston and Chamberlain, and the two bodies were gone."

I thought of the worst possibility. "Jeanne may have been kidnapped."

Lambert smirked. "Yeah, and maybe the tooth fairy will leave a note under my pillow tonight telling me where they've taken her."

Drakesford shot Lambert a look that told me the FBI agent annoyed him.

I turned to Drakesford. "What about Chamberlain? Is he part of some group?"

Again, Lambert jumped in. "Sure, he's part of some group. But without his body or his personal papers, I have no way of tracing him. I've only got a name because a medic searched through his wallet for a medical alert."

"You have the gun, don't you?"

"The gun? Yes, we have the gun. Complete with prints from fingers so washed by acid the patterns look like octopus suckers. Did I mention there's no driver's license issued to a Caucasian named Sidney Chamberlain in Vermont?"

"No."

"So the trail ends where it'll have to begin. With Jeanne Everston. Now you gonna help us?"

I'd been overwhelmed with incomprehensible information. The Jeanne Everston I knew this morning no longer existed. "Yes, but I don't expect to hear from her."

Drakesford shook his head. "Son, in this business, learn to expect the unexpected."

I watched them get into the elevator. Drakesford had tried to be friendly again. He said he'd check with me in the morning and keep me posted. Guess I was back on the team. I went straight to a phone behind the nurse's station and called home. There must have been at least ten messages from reporters wanting interviews and another ten from friends worried about me. Even wiseguy Kevin Ferris phoned asking if he could help.

I walked down the hall, confused and feeling sorry for myself. What was Jeanne up to? Why'd she been in my house? Would I find her there tomorrow?

The door to seven-eleven opened and Katherine's mother slipped out. She saw me and forced a smile. Her eyes were red and puffy.

"Are you all right, Mrs. Thompson?"

She half-laughed, half-cried, and wiped tears from her cheek with the sleeve of her blouse. "I haven't been all right for a long time, Gene. A long time. Surely God's got a heart. He's got a heart for my little girl."

"I'm sure he does."

She came over and wrapped her arms around me. "You are so special, Gene. It's like God's chosen you to be here for Katherine."

God's chosen. The phrase echoed in my head, spoken by two very different people, both of whom had pulled me close to them. One had threatened me with a gun; the other thanked me with a mother's love.

I returned to my room and called Dad in Chicago. It didn't matter if the phone were bugged because I'd be expected to make that call. We talked for about an hour and I didn't mention my encounter with Drakesford and FBI Agent Lambert. I encouraged Dad to stay on his business schedule. When we said good night, I felt whipped. Although it was only nine o'clock, I felt like I'd been up for days.

Clean towels and one of those villainous hospital nightgowns had been left folded on the foot of the bed. I took a hot shower that washed both the sweat and tension away. The nightgown was skimpy but more comfortable than sleeping in my clothes. I kept my underwear on as a barrier against total embarrassment in case some nurse came in by mistake and I had kicked off the covers.

I tumbled down into dreamless sleep as soon as my head hit the pillow. Then, from far away, someone whispered my name. I struggled against the sound, wanting to stay safely in the cocoon of unconsciousness. The voice became louder, breath tickled my ear, and I felt hair brush across my forehead. My eyes snapped open. Inches above me, suspended in the night shadows, loomed the face of Jeanne Everston.

"Wake up. We've got to get out of here."

11

"What time is it?" I asked the question because I was too bewildered to say anything else.

"A few minutes after three." She backed away from the bed and nearly disappeared as her black jeans and pullover merged with the darkness. She held out a paper bag. "Here's a change of clothes."

I sat up and checked that the hospital gown covered my bare thighs before throwing off the sheet. "Jeanne, you're wanted by the police. The FBI. I can't go with you."

"You can't stay. Not here. This is big, Gene. My father spent two years tracking the source of the conspiracy."

"What conspiracy? The transplant list? The donors? There's an FBI agent who can help."

"No. We'd never live to testify. I've got to get more evidence before we go public. You want to get dressed in the bathroom or should I wait in there? I can't stand in the hall."

The whole scene made no sense. Her urgent

demand that we leave was forcing me to move before I could think. Things were not adding up. Why had the bodies disappeared? How did she know the man who killed her father had a computer disk? Her actions were as conspiratorial as anything Drakesford and Lambert had done. How much did I really know about Jeanne Everston? I sensed other discrepancies lurking in the back of my mind.

"No. I'm not going. Jeanne, you're in shock. God knows you should be, but running away does neither of us any good. Do you have a relative or minister you can talk to?" I didn't know if she was religious, but there had to be a way to calm her down. "Maybe a teacher? Mr. Wallingford?"

"I've got help, Gene. It's you I'm worried about. You're alone. You don't know how alone." She stepped forward and dropped the bag in my lap. "If you'll get dressed, I can show you the proof here in the hospital. Then if you want to come back, you can. If you want to call the police, I won't stop you." She bent down until her face was next to mine. "Will you trust me that far?"

Before I could open my mouth to answer, she kissed me on the lips, extinguishing any flame of resistance. After all, it wasn't like she was asking me to leave the hospital.

When I opened the bag in the bathroom, I discovered Jeanne had raided not just my closet but my dresser as well. Clean underwear, black socks, black jeans with my belt already threaded through the loops, and a navy blue T-shirt turned me into her fashion twin. She'd also brought my old black Reeboks to replace the newer, silver Nikes. I was embarrassed to think of her going through my things, especially since I'd left my room as trashed as the bleachers after a high school football game. Still, she'd picked the right stuff. All we needed was to coat our faces with soot and we'd be a pair of cat burglars.

"You check the hall," she told me. "They won't think it's unusual you're not sleeping well in a hospital. If no one's looking, scoot across to the stairwell as fast and quietly as you can."

"Were you this careful when you broke into my house?"

"Glad you didn't have a security system."

"Obviously, we should get one." I took a deep breath, trying to relax before making the dash. "I was stunned when Agent Lambert said you called from my phone."

I cracked the door open. Jeanne put her palm flat against it and pushed it shut.

"What?" she whispered.

"Your call. To the playroom."

"Gene, I made that call from a payphone. I didn't go to your house till midnight."

"You're sure?"

"What do you mean I'm sure? I know where I was. I didn't want the call to be traced."

"Why would Lambert lie? When they caught me on the phone with you, I said I was checking messages. Lambert checked Caller I.D. and read off my home number. How would he know my number?"

"He probably knew your home phone number. Maybe because he requested a wiretap."

"But that doesn't explain why he'd lie to Detective Drakesford. And he knew that I knew he was lying."

Suddenly, I felt very alone. How did I know Jeanne was telling the truth? She may have said she called from a phone booth just to make me suspicious of Lambert, to make me believe her paranoia. Had I fallen down the rabbit hole? Like Alice in Wonderland, I found things becoming "curiouser and curiouser." Everything was turning upside-down. Except in this Wonderland, people were getting killed.

"He's getting something to hold over you," Jeanne said. "Something he can use to control you."

"Control me to do what?"

"Probably something he doesn't want the other detective to know about. I think the sooner you get away from him, the better." She took her hand off the door and stepped back.

The corridor was empty. A child whimpered in a room down the hall. Overhead, a flickering fluorescent bulb droned. As I walked out, Jeanne squeezed beside me, keeping my body between her and anyone who might turn the corner or come out of a room. When we were safely in the stairwell, she caught my arm and whispered, "Stay close. We're going to take the back way to the lab. Security is tight. I'll have to use my father's pass-code to get through the unguarded door."

We trekked down seven flights of stairs and left the main hospital through the emergency room. No one paid us any attention. Then we strolled along an interconnecting sidewalk toward the research tower. The pathway was trimmed with blooming pansies and lit by a string of electric lanterns. Jeanne took my arm in hers and snuggled against my side. Just a couple of teenagers out for a romantic walk at four in the morning.

We veered away from the main entrance and followed an asphalt utility lane to the chiller units which send tons of cold air into the super-computer rooms scattered throughout the building. Its high-pitched whine pierced our ears and drowned out anything less than a shout. Jeanne pointed to a door just beyond where the giant air conduits penetrated the wall.

An electronic lock required both a magnetic-striped card and a numerical sequence punched into the digital pad. Jeanne's fingers flew across the keys and I heard the metallic click as the bolts snapped free. Once inside, she led me to a second door on the right and into the dimly lit back stairwell.

"Only four flights this time," she said.

"Yeah, all up."

We came into the Center for Infertility and Reproductive Studies through a storage room. Jeanne again took my hand as we navigated through piles of boxes and rows of filing cabinets. Her palm was sweaty. Her nerves had to be stretched to the breaking point. If she knew where the light switch was located, she didn't turn it on. Only the glow of a wall-mounted safety lamp kept us from stumbling through the maze of obstacles.

The next room was completely dark except for green spots of light coming from what I figured to be running computer terminals. Any monitors must have been turned off. Jeanne closed the door from the storage room behind us and announced, "Gene and Jeanne."

Immediately, the overhead fluorescent bulbs came on at full intensity. At the far wall, an old man with bushy white hair and mustache removed his hand from the light switch. He peered at us over half-frame reading glasses and smiled like a child on Christmas morning.

"Gene Adamson," Jeanne said, "meet Randall Weaver, the world's oldest computer geek."

If Albert Einstein were reincarnated as an elf, he would be Randall Weaver. The man bounced over to us with surprising energy. His ocean-blue eyes looked me up and down like I were some fascinating specimen he could add to his collection. "Yes, yes," he said to himself. "Gene Adamson. A delight. A true delight." He turned to Jeanne. "You were gone so long I was afraid I'd fall asleep sitting in the dark."

"Why were you in the dark?" I asked.

"Because I was afraid I'd fall asleep sitting in the light."

Maybe I am in Wonderland, I thought, or a Dr. Seuss book. He saw the bewildered expression on my face.

"If I fell asleep in the light," he explained, "the security guard may notice when he makes his rounds every hour. He doesn't come in this room, but he can see the crack under the door."

"And we've got twenty-five minutes before he comes again," Jeanne prompted. "Show Gene what we've found."

"Yes, yes." He clapped his hands together. "Let's

get to it."

We followed him to the largest computer station in the room. Randall Weaver clicked the power button on the monitor and a page of numerical data appeared in columns on the screen. A red banner across the top of the columns read "SECURED SITE – NOPC."

"I know what you're thinking, young man. Who's this old geezer hacking away in the domain of the twenty-year-olds. Well, I was there with Johnny von Neumann when he created the architecture for the modern computer. 1945. You know what I told him?"

"No." I had no idea who Johnny von Neumann was.

"Don't think big, Johnny, think small. And, by jiminy, I was right." He gestured to the screen. "The computing power in this unit would have filled this whole building in 1945."

"Hello, Randall," Jeanne said impatiently. "Welcome to the present."

"Yes, yes, the present. Well, what you see is a page from NOPC."

"What's that?" I asked.

"National Organ Procurement Center," Jeanne said.

"This list is composed in descending order of critical priority," Mr. Weaver explained. "The numbers are coded identification for the individuals waiting for transplants." He held up a CD. "And this is the decoding software."

"The disk Chamberlain took?" I asked.

"Yes," Jeanne said. "My father and Randall had figured out what was happening and Randall duplicated the program."

"But someone latched onto my efforts and realized their sinister scheme was being exposed."

"Scheme to do what?"

Without saying another word, Randall Weaver popped the disk into the computer. An icon for the CD drive appeared in the lower right corner of the monitor, over the data sheet. Mr. Weaver moved his cursor to the icon and double-clicked. The identify-cation numbers became names. At the top of the list, I read THOMPSON, KATHERINE A. Then he moved the cursor to a MCGUIRE, TANYA six or seven places down. He double-clicked again. Nothing happened.

"What's the big deal about revealing identities of children needing heart transplants?" I asked.

"Nothing," he said. "The big deal is concealing, not revealing." He ejected the CD and the database returned to numbers.

"Isn't Katherine's number the same?" I asked.

"The top priority number is certainly the same. Now, if I look for a match to a donor," he re-inserted the disk and clicked on the icon, "the computer gives me—"

MCGUIRE, TANYA. Katherine's code had been linked to a different name.

I could only sputter "That's . . . That's . . ."

"Murder would be an appropriate word," Jeanne said. "Killing someone by denying them their rightful donor organ, attaching another name to their code."

"Who's Tanya McGuire?"

"I don't know," Weaver said. "A name I picked at

random from the list. But earlier, Katherine Thompson's name had been switch-linked to a Robert Cantero, a twelve-year-old boy who underwent a heart transplant operation yesterday afternoon."

So this was who received the organ Mrs. Malkovski thought should have come to Katherine.

Weaver waved the disk in front of my face. "And Robert Cantero's father, James, is a high-ranking official in the FBI."

The light bulb went off in my head. "That's why you're afraid to go to the police?"

"Until we've got a complete trail. From the source of the name switch to a money tie between the organ recipient and that source."

"How long will it take?"

"A few days. A hacker leaves a signature which isn't easy to delete if one knows how to follow it. He had to cover this intrusion into the NOPC system and reinstate Katherine Thompson to her proper position. But we ourselves have been discovered. Chamberlain was an assassin sent to eliminate what the conspiracy thought was one doctor, John Everston, finding the truth."

"How'd they know it was Dr. Everston?"

"Because I penetrated NOPC from the computer network in this laboratory." He looked at Jeanne. "And because Dr. Everston's wife died while awaiting a transplant. She was herself a victim of the conspiracy."

THE PRESENT

12

Don't say I didn't warn you about becoming impatient. I can't explain everything at once. Yet, as I look back, I'm impatient with myself for arriving at the truth so slowly. "You can't see the forest for the trees" is the phrase which comes to mind. Double-branched trees were popping up everywhere: Jeanne has a mother who dies while awaiting a transplant and my mother dies needing a transplant; little Katherine is pre-empted by the son of an FBI official and the FBI is hunting for Jeanne; Dr. Everston uncovers a plot to manipulate a list of prioritized organ recipients and Dr. Everston's killer tells me I'm on a list; Detective Drakesford and Paul Lockaby lie to the press about my condition and keep me in the hospital and FBI Agent Jason Lambert lies to Drakesford about the phone trace and keeps him unaware of my own lie.

I was so fixated on discovering how individual events fit into an intricate pattern I didn't consider the significance that such a pattern even appeared to exist. "You can't see the forest for the trees" has another possible interpretation: "You can't see that there is no forest for the trees." If the trees have been skillfully planted, you might think you're in a forest when, in fact, a few steps down the right path can open up a whole new horizon. However, I assumed I was in a forest which I couldn't see and I kept looking for more trees to identify. Two critical ones needed to be placed in the pattern: why had Jeanne and Randall Weaver taken the bodies and why should a dying murderer tell me I was on a list? As convincing as Randall Weaver's demonstration had been, I didn't want to go into hiding until I knew how these "trees" fit into the forest of my imagination.

So the questions I wanted to ask Jeanne in private . . .

THE PAST

13

. . . now required answers that she had to give in front of Randall Weaver before I would leave the hospital.

"Jeanne, I don't understand why you took the bodies."

She hesitated, looking to Weaver for guidance. The old man shrugged as if to say go ahead, there's no point in hiding anything.

"After my father was shot, I came back here. I knew when Chamberlain tried to kill me, he wasn't just some religious nut. He wanted to eliminate anyone who threatened the conspiracy. That meant he must have found this CD while we were in the lecture hall."

"Where were you?" I asked Weaver.

"I only come in at night. Whenever we ran into others, Dr. Everston told them I was a computer tech who worked after hours."

"Someone had gone through our files," Jeanne said. "I thought the CD might still be on Chamberlain's body."

"That only explains why you wanted his things," I

said.

"We wanted more than that," Weaver said. "We aren't without resources. By taking his body, we could run our own check on fingerprints, body markings, and other distinguishing physical features. Otherwise, a corrupt FBI agent could arrange to either hide or fabricate any background he chose for Mr. Sidney Chamberlain."

"And what have you learned?"

"Nothing yet," Weaver admitted, "except that his prints have been eradicated."

His statement matched what I learned from Drakesford and Lambert. The assassin had taken great pains to conceal his personal history.

"And your father?" I asked Jeanne.

"Since we needed to take Chamberlain's body, I asked that my father be removed as well. Then, when the danger has passed, I can arrange for a proper burial."

"Who are you that you can conjure up orderlies and ether on an hour's notice?"

"We are a small, tight-knit group willing to take risks. We can't trust our government, our law enforcement agencies, or our medical institutions. We are extremely vulnerable until we have enough conclusive evidence to convince the press and the general public. Only then will we be safe."

His argument fit the facts: Dr. Everston had been murdered, Katherine Thompson did not receive her heart, FBI Agent Lambert lied, and I had seen the CD invade the National Organ Procurement Center database and alter the priority list.

"If everything you say is true, then why me?"

"Why you?" Weaver asked.

"Yes, why did Chamberlain tell me I was on the list? I'm not waiting for an organ donor. I can't believe he was delusional."

"I don't think he was," Jeanne said. "I think he knew he was dying and wanted to warn you. A final act of kindness."

"Warn me about what?"

"The second list," Weaver said. "The one that completes the transaction. The conspiracy moves a name to the top of the critical candidates." He pointed to the computer monitor. "You've seen how that works. There's also a list of potential donors, those compassionate citizens and family members who have been screened, tissue-typed, and entered into a database, the way you were for your mother. You, Gene, may be a harvestable product, a compatible donor who matches the medical need of someone willing to give money or power for your body parts. Why should the conspiracy stop at sentencing to death those who are pushed down the list? You might be marked for delivery to an anxious customer, my friend. Someone's playing God with your life. That's Chamberlain's second list. He may have even planned to arrange for your availability himself."

The chill rippled up from the base of my spine. The evil of such a scheme overwhelmed me. Securing a place at the top of a recipient list was bad enough, but to think an organized hit squad would create the "accidental deaths" of matching donors smacked of Nazi atrocities.

"You're not safe anywhere else," Jeanne said. She took hold of both my hands and felt them tremble. "Won't you come with us?"

I remembered a very important rule from last year's Biology class. When an organism is confronted with danger, there are two instinctive choices: fight or flight. I could stay in the hospital and face an unknown enemy or I could flee with this beautiful girl who faced me now.

"I'll have to call Dad at some point. Let him know I'm safe."

"We can work that out," Weaver said. "Where is he?"

"The Sheraton in Chicago, but I'd like to call him myself."

"I hope that'll be very soon." Weaver glanced at his watch. "The guard will be by in a few minutes. Let's get out of here."

Jeanne led me away like a lamb to the slaughter.

14

We emerged through the side door and into the steady whine of the chillers. Humid air clung to us like invisible steam. Dawn was less than an hour away and the eastern sky now held the hint of gray. Against the faint light, I could see the bare concrete structure of the new Levine Children's Hospital rising twelve stories. In another year, our facility on the seventh floor would be replaced by this miracle of modern technology and community support.

Jeanne started following Randall Weaver up the hill toward the employee parking lot, but I pulled her back.

"I've got to go to my room," I said. "My clothes and guitar are still there."

"Too risky. The nurses will take care of them."

"No," I insisted. "It's too risky to leave them. What will the staff think? Either I wandered off delirious or I was abducted. The police will start searching for me."

By this time, Weaver noticed we had stopped. He

motioned us to hurry, then jogged back when I stood my ground.

"What's wrong now?" he asked impatiently.

"We're going to be safer if I tell the duty nurse I'm leaving. I'll just say I can't sleep and I'm going home to lay low and keep away from reporters for a few days. She knows Dr. Lockaby gave me permission to take time off. She'll pass that on to the dayshift and no one, especially the police, will have reason to think otherwise."

"That makes sense," Weaver agreed.

"Where should I meet you?" I asked.

"No, I don't want you trying to find us by yourself," Jeanne said. "I've got a better idea. Randall can take my car. I'll wait and we can ride together."

I left Jeanne at the edge of the parking lot and managed to enter the hospital through the emergency room without anyone stopping me. My room had been undisturbed. I stuffed my dirty clothes and extra shoes into a pillow case, figuring housekeeping wouldn't miss one. Setting the bundle and my guitar case behind the door, I walked down the hall to tell the nurse I wanted to leave before any reporters arrived.

Luckily, I found no one at the station. I scribbled a quick note on the back of a meal menu card and taped it to a computer screen. I looked at the words for a few seconds and realized I had crossed into new territory. Now I was lying. This was different from the hospital and police putting out misleading statements. I was consciously being deceitful, telling the people I worked with something that wasn't true. There was a good chance they'd discover my lies if I remained in hiding for more than several days. What would they think of me then?

I became angry that I was forced into this position, angry that I'd lost control of my own life, and angry that a little girl down the hall may die because her chance for life was being stolen. That gave my anger purpose and what others thought of me didn't matter. I had one goal: help catch the people behind this evil.

On my way back to pick up my things, I peeked in on Katherine. The light from the hall illuminated the room enough to reveal her mother sleeping in the fold-out chair at the foot of the bed. A single linen sheet served as a blanket and her hands clenched its hem close to her chin. The lines of worry had magically disappeared from her face. Perhaps, in Mrs. Thompson's dream world, her daughter ran and swam like any ten-year-old. There would be birthdays and graduations, proms and college boards, and, most importantly, a future.

Katherine, too, slept peacefully on her side. But her lips looked a little bluer, her body thinner, and her condition more desperate. I made a second promise to her. I would do whatever I could to help Mr. Weaver make sure she wasn't passed over again and I would be here for her birthday and the day she got her new heart and her new life.

When I returned to the parking lot, I offered to let Jeanne drive the Toyota since she knew our destination.

"No," she said. "You were careful enough to leave the hospital without drawing attention to yourself.

Why chance someone seeing me drive your car? I'll slump down in the passenger's seat until we're on the back streets."

She stayed curled up below the window until we reached Dilworth Road, a neighborhood lane bordered by towering water oaks. Their canopy completely blocked the sky and hid any trace of the approaching dawn.

I stopped at the curb and looked around. All the houses on the block were dark. "Where do we go from here?"

She took a minute to figure out where we were, then nodded with approval. "We can stay on the side roads to MacDonald Avenue. Randall's house is on the end towards South Boulevard."

"Is that where we're staying?"

"I hope so. It should be safe. At least long enough for us to get everything out in the open."

MacDonald Avenue was less than five minutes away. We met only one car coming the other way, a convertible whose driver was too busy tossing the morning paper into the yards of subscribers to pay us any attention. The avenue was populated by brick or clapboard bungalows, mostly two bedrooms, with fern-adorned porches across the front. The neighborhood's closeness to uptown had sent selling prices skyward and young working couples moved in as the older generation either passed on to retirement centers or simply passed on.

"It's the second brick house on the left," Jeanne said. "Pull into the driveway."

I swung the Toyota onto the concrete that led to a

two-car garage. Mr. Weaver must have been watching from the darkened house and hit his remote opener because the door automatically lifted, revealing Jeanne's Miata and an empty space beside it.

As we entered the back door, a light came on in the kitchen.

"Welcome to Randall Weaver's all-night diner." The old man held up a black frying pan and spatula. "Scrambled eggs, toast, and O.J. is the specialty of the house. We'll have breakfast, then get some sleep. Jeanne, put him in my room. You take the guest bed and I'll use the sofa."

"I'm not going to throw you out of your own bedroom," I protested. "And I'm too keyed-up to sleep."

"Look, Gene, we've got a lot of work to do and very little time. I want the sofa because it's by the computer and the computer's set to notify me if there's any change in the list. You want that little girl to get her heart, don't you?"

"Yes."

"And we want to break up the conspiracy behind Dr. Everston's murder?"

"Of course."

"Then let me get the evidence and you get some rest. Now, how do you want your eggs—scrambled or scrambled?"

I had to laugh. He looked like he would bop me on the head with the skillet if I gave the wrong answer.

"I'll have some of each."

"Good. Go in and get settled."

Mr. Weaver's bedroom was down a short hall

from the kitchen. A bathroom separated it from the guest room.

"Why don't you wash up while I help him," Jeanne said. "Otherwise, he could turn the toast into charcoal."

His bedroom reminded me of my grandmother Downing's house. Nother Mama, as I called her, was my mom's mother. Each summer I'd spent a week at her home in the western North Carolina town of Brevard. I had great memories of her home by a bold stream and acres of mountain woods to explore. Nother Mama died five years ago, the last of my grandparents. This room gave comfort because there I'd slept in a bed like Mr. Weaver's, a high-framed single mattress with a heavy wooden headboard.

Weaver's dresser was like the one in my room at Nother Mama's as well. Four large drawers were stacked from the bottom and a pair of smaller ones were side by side at the top. The surface of the dresser bore the scratches of years of coins, cufflinks, and pens left on them. I knew because these items lay scattered between several pewter-framed photographs.

The pictures were even older than the ones at my grandmother's. I lifted one which had turned yellowish-brown over the years and stared into the face of a boy about my own age. He wore the basic uniform of a Union infantryman. The resemblance to Mr. Weaver was striking and clearly told of a familial tie. Perhaps a great grandfather or other ancestor had come South after the war. Two other portraits included a woman with the same boy, now a young man. He looked to be in his early twenties in both, but the woman looked like a teenager in one and a forty-year-old in the other. They had to be mother and daughter and I wondered what their relationship was to the Union soldier.

The smell of toast and bacon broke me out of my speculations. I picked up the towel and wash cloth I found folded at the foot of the bed and went into the bathroom to clean away the weariness of the past night.

Jeanne had set three places at a white enamel table in a corner of the kitchen.

"Have a seat," she said. "Your order will be right up."

I squeezed into the chair against the wall, leaving Weaver and Jeanne the more accessible ones. She brought me a large orange juice to keep me going while our cooking host finished preparations. A few minutes later, we all sat before plates of scrambled eggs, crisp bacon, and diagonally cut slices of whole wheat toast.

"Sorry there's no coffee," Weaver said. "I don't drink it myself and it's not the best idea if we're going to get some sleep." He slid a bottle of ketchup toward me. "Want this?"

"For my eggs?"

"Sure."

"So, you're a Yankee," I joked. "At least that's what my Dad says. Only Yankees like ketchup on eggs."

"Guilty."

"How long have you lived here?"

"A couple years. I retired here. Like the climate.

Four seasons but without the Yankee winter."

"Who's the Union soldier on your dresser?"

"You noticed him, huh? Jeanne said you'd worked on a Civil War project together. That was my namesake, Randall J. Weaver of Pennsylvania. Saw action at Gettysburg and lived to tell about it. Born July 3, 1846, and celebrated his seventeenth birthday looking out over a sea of advancing rebels."

"And the women in the other pictures?"

The pride in Mr. Weaver's eyes changed to sadness. He looked at Jeanne for a few seconds, then said, "His bride and life-long love. Helen was her name."

"Was the older woman her mother?"

"Mother?" Mr. Weaver hesitated as if he had forgotten about that photograph. "Oh, yes, and she was every bit the lady as her daughter."

"Randall's a genealogy buff," Jeanne said. "He helped me with those personal stories for our pre-sentation."

The old man winked at me. "I'll spare you for now. Don't want you nodding off at the table."

I did feel tired. Just sitting down and calming down let me know how exhausted I was. We finished breakfast and I was ready for a couple hours of sleep.

I closed the bedroom door behind me. The one window on the opposite wall wasn't covered with curtains, but with a cream-colored, pull-down shade that effectively blocked the daylight. The house did have one important modern feature: central air conditioning. The air blowing through the overhead vent would keep the room from getting hot and stuffy as the temperature soared outside.

I pulled the white spread down to the foot of the bed, slipped off my shoes and lay down on top of a sky-blue cotton blanket. For a few minutes, I was aware of the whisper of cool air coming from the vent. Then, oblivion.

I awoke in two stages. First, my mind crawled up out of the abyss of unconsciousness. I became aware of my sleeping body and heard my own rhythmic breathing, but I didn't have the energy or desire to open my eyes. The sound of voices filtered into my semi-consciousness. Somewhere, in a dream, a man and a woman were talking. I could make out the words but placed no significance on the context.

"He's still out," said a woman. "How much did you put in the juice?"

"Just three Benadryl," answered the man. "He's very tired from staying up all night."

"What should we do?" asked the woman.

"Stay with the plan. You pick up the old one. It's important he see the boy as soon as possible. We can't continue much longer."

"And you?"

"I'll wait here and keep him occupied. I'm expecting a call from the crematorium."

"He's no fool," said the woman.

"He can't afford to be."

Somewhere I heard a creak of footsteps and a door closing, then I dreamed I was singing songs on the eve of Gettysburg with Jeanne and a Union infantryman.

I awoke with a start, sensing that a great deal of

time had passed. My wristwatch told me it was two-thirty. My mouth and nose were dry and I wanted nothing more than a cold glass of water. I sat up on the edge of the bed and ran my fingers through the tangled curls of my hair. I tried massaging the grogginess out of my head. I remembered I was in Mr. Weaver's house and began to reconstruct the pieces of my dream. The voices had not been faceless fantasies of sleep. Jeanne and Mr. Weaver had been talking, probably in this room. Talking about me and Benadryl, an antihistamine for allergies and the main ingredient in over-the-counter sleeping pills. No wonder I craved water. And what couldn't they continue much longer? Their private investigation of organ-donor abuses? Hiding from a corrupt FBI agent? I had a right to know and I intended to ask them.

I went to the door and turned the knob. It was locked. My heart started pounding harder. I'd been drugged and locked in this room by a girl I trusted, a girl I was beginning to think of as more than a friend. Now, all I wanted was to get out of the house and call Dad. Fly to Chicago if I had to. I crossed the bedroom to the window and grabbed the pull-tassel. The spring-lock released, and as the spindle reeled in the shade, I saw my plight all too clearly. The window was covered by iron bars.

15

My first instinct was to break out the glass and start screaming. Someone would hear. Someone would call the police. But would help come before I was silenced? If I panicked, I'd lose any advantage I held of surprise. Mr. Weaver and Jeanne didn't know I was awake. Perhaps Jeanne had left to "pick up the old one" as Mr. Weaver said and he felt more secure keeping me confined in the bedroom.

I knelt down, looked through the old-fashioned keyhole, and saw what I hoped to see. Black nothing. A key blocked the light. I had the chance to go from amateur magician to escape artist. The plan wasn't original. I'd seen it in an old black and white detective movie where the hero pushed the key out of the lock so it fell on a newspaper he'd slipped under the door. Then he pulled the paper back inside and got the key.

Searching the bedroom, I found neither a newspaper nor a magazine. My brain raced to improvise something else. Weaver's closet contained a few worn sport coats and mismatched pants. I dumped one outfit on the floor and bent its wire hanger into an elongated diamond. I put on my running shoes and went to work.

For the second time in a few hours, I stripped a pillowcase off a bed. Using the coat hanger as a prod, I pushed the rectangular pillowcase under the door and along the hardwood floor until only the hem was on my side. Then I lifted the wire and retrieved it without disturbing my spread net. I straightened the curved end to fit in the keyhole. Inserting it, I pushed gently, feeling for the slightest give that let me know the key was moving. If I applied too much pressure, the key could pop out and bounce off the pillowcase, leaving me trapped with a clear sign on the hall floor that I was aware of my predicament. The key yielded and I slowly advanced the wire. With a dull clink, the key hit the floor. I didn't wait to hear if footsteps approached. I reeled in my catch.

The lock gave a faint click as I turned the key. Stepping out in the hall, I looked toward the guestroom. Both Jeanne's door and the one to the bathroom were closed. My best exit lay back through the kitchen to the garage, but I wasn't sure where Weaver was. I didn't want to have a physical confrontation with an old man. And he could even be armed. Then I heard him cough in the bathroom. If Jeanne were gone, my way was clear. I locked the bedroom door behind me and left the key in the latch. Perhaps he wouldn't realize I'd gone.

I stopped in the kitchen. What proof would I have that I'd been held against my will? Or that Jeanne and Mr. Weaver were themselves in a conspiracy? I took a chance and went through the dining room to the living room where I found the computer by the sofa just as Weaver had described. The list of coded transplant recipients appeared on the monitor and I realized what was wrong. I popped the CD out of the drive and grabbed two more that were stacked beside the keyboard.

The wind snapped the back screen door out of my hand as I opened it. Thunder rumbled from dark clouds coming from the west. Soon one of July's vicious storms would cut a drenching path through the city. I stuck the three CDs in my hip pocket and ran for the garage. The double door wouldn't budge. Peering through the window, I saw my Toyota alone inside. The car may as well have been parked on the moon.

Thunder cracked again, this time closer. I debated going back in the house and trying to find the remote opener. The decision was made for me.

"Gene, what are you doing?" Mr. Weaver stood in his stocking feet at the back door. His white hair blew so high in the gusty wind I could see the brown roots. He extended his empty hands in a visible appeal. "Come back in the house."

"Why'd you lock me in your room?"

"I locked me out of your room. I can be forgetful and I didn't want to barge in while you were sleeping. I went in just now to check on you. All you had to do was call me."

"And the bars on the window?"

"I've been burglarized three times. There are bars on all the windows on the backside. Come in. I'll show you."

A poem sprang into my mind. "Won't you come into my parlor? said the spider to the fly." I remembered the fly ended up as dinner.

"No. You haven't been honest with me. You're not monitoring the transplant list. The computer's not even hooked up to a phone or cable line. You're just pulling data off these CDs." I reached in my pocket and pulled out the three disks.

"Give me those!" he barked and even the thunder wasn't as threatening. "You don't know what you're doing." He started walking toward me.

"So you want me to wait around for the old one. Why? So he can hypnotize me into forgetting how you tricked me?"

"So he can open your eyes to the truth. You belong with us, Gene."

He kept coming and I retreated down the driveway. Then he sprinted, this seventy-year-old man ran at me like a linebacker after a quarterback. I was so startled he nearly caught me. I darted to my left, out of his grasp, and ran across his front yard onto Mac-Donald Avenue. I can't imagine what any neighbors would have thought to see us, a high school boy running full-out with an old man in stocking feet matching him stride for stride.

The heavens opened and the deluge fell. I crossed the street and looked for an unfenced backyard where I could cut through to the next block. The uneven ground and exposed tree roots gave Mr. Weaver's shoeless feet trouble and he lagged behind. I dashed down a driveway and out onto Euclid Avenue. Brakes squealed and I turned to see a forest-green Miata skid to a stop a few yards away. Behind its wheel sat Jeanne. Her face was contorted by the scare of the near-miss. In the passenger's seat, a young, dark-skinned man stared at me with liquid brown eyes. His expression was as calm and inscrutable as the Sphinx.

I froze for only an instant, then ran past them. Before Jeanne could turn her car around, I was out of sight.

16

The storm raged for another half hour. I took shelter behind two garbage cans in a carport hidden from the street. I figured the residents of the house wouldn't venture out to their Buick until the rain eased and they certainly weren't about to make a trash run.

Safety in my hiding place was little comfort. My life had taken a dangerous turn. Soaked to the skin, I crouched on a cold concrete floor while lightning flashed around me. I had ten dollars in my wallet, my hospital I.D., and three computer disks, one of which a man had killed for. If I called the police, I could wind up in an office with Lambert, a man I didn't trust. Jeanne, Mr. Weaver, and the FBI agent had all lied to me. What if I now knew enough to be a threat to one of them? I wished I were a real magician and could make them disappear. But, even the great Harry Potter couldn't vaporize his evil adversary. What chance did I have in the real world?

In my mind, I replayed the Miata skidding toward me. Had the fear on Jeanne's face been for my life or because I'd escaped? Who was the mysterious companion? The young man looked Indian or Pakistani. Had they been on their way to pick up "the old one?"

There was no way I could learn these answers wandering around Charlotte like a half-drowned kitten. Yet, I couldn't go home because the FBI was certainly watching my house. Jeanne knew my closest friends—Robbie, Diane, Tyler—and possibly had them under observation. I couldn't call them. Mr. Weaver said his group was small and determined, but how small and how determined? Did they have enough members to dispatch them to Charlotte in search of one Gene Adamson?

I could think of two options open to me and both could be pursued. If I reached Dad, he could book me a ticket for Chicago. I'd feel safer there rather than bringing him here. Perhaps flying out of Greensboro or Columbia, South Carolina, each about ninety minutes away, would increase the odds for eluding discovery.

Second, I needed to learn more about the disks I'd stolen. Maybe Mr. Weaver lied about monitoring the transplant list from his house, but that didn't mean such a conspiracy didn't exist at the hospital. If these CDs held the truth, I could bypass the police and take my story to the press. *The Charlotte Observer* here or the *Tribune* in Chicago. Nothing would happen to me once the media got hold of the facts.

The rain began to subside and so did my panic. I left the luxury of my garbage-can hideaway and started walking through the drizzle toward East Boulevard. A

CIRCLE K convenience store provided a payphone and a quick escape route back into the neighborhood should I be spotted. The cashier changed my ten into a fistful of coins.

The long distance operator connected me to the Sheraton in Chicago and I got the voice-mail for my father's room. "Dad. I've got to talk to you. You can't reach me at home or the hospital. Can you be in your room at seven tonight? I'll phone then." I hung up, hoping I sounded serious but not scared. Yesterday, I had been the one who told my father not to come home, that I'd be all right. Now he'd feel guilty that he hadn't taken the first flight back.

The rain stopped. The sun lifted the water up as steam and the air became a suffocating wall of heat. It was almost four. I needed a place to hide until seven, a place where I could read the data on the CDs. The main branch of the public library had a state-of-the-art link to the internet. Computer terminals could be reserved and data retrieved. The only problem lay in the three-mile trek uptown. I looked on the bright side. My clothes would have plenty of time to dry.

Before I started my hike, I placed a call to retrieve messages from the answering machine. A wiretap may reveal this payphone number, but I'd be gone before anyone responded. Four beeps indicated four new messages.

The first, at 9:05 A.M.: "Gene? This is Detective Drakesford. We were surprised you left the hospital so early this morning. Please call me. Just want to make sure you're okay."

The second, at 3:09 P.M.: "Gene. Agent Lambert

here. We need to talk. I'd prefer you contact me at my direct cell number, 202-555-0801. I have confidential information which needs to stay between you and me. I'll be waiting."

The third, at 3:26 P.M.: "Gene, it's Jeanne. There's been a terrible misunderstanding. I know why you ran, but you've put yourself in danger. Come back. I can explain everything."

The fourth, at 3:52 P.M., only a few minutes ago: "Hey, Goober, this is Kevin. Saw your ugly mug on TV last night. Broke the screen. No, I was just checking in again, you know, like if you need something. I'm cell-phone challenged, but you can get me at home, 905-0105. If you wanna, you know, wanna talk."

So I was back to Goober. Kevin was good to call, but he couldn't resist a little jab. It was a personality trait that kept him distant from the rest of us. No one really disliked Kevin. He was smart and prepared in class, but he always had an edge of sarcasm that went beyond being funny. Like he tried too hard or something.

That's when the idea hit me. Kevin Ferris was a loner. No one considered him as best or even close friend and Jeanne would never suspect him as someone I'd turn to for help. Time grew short. If my home line were tapped, this payphone location might now be identified. I had a few minutes at most, but Kevin should still be at his house.

A woman answered "Hello" in an ancient, whispery voice. I thought I'd dialed the wrong number. I didn't know anything about Kevin's family, but this person sounded like she must be eighty.

"Is Kevin there?"

"Just a minute, please. He's fixing tea." She set the receiver down with a clunk.

I had trouble picturing Kevin brewing afternoon tea like some Brit. I heard the woman faintly call his name, then the phone was silent.

A few minutes ticked by. Cars pulled in and out of the CIRCLE K. One dark blue sedan turned off East Boulevard and headed for me. I nearly bolted for fear a government vehicle would pin me against the wall. Then I noticed the handicapped permit dangling from the rearview mirror as the car slowly crept into the reserved space in front of me. I relaxed as an elderly man hobbled into the store on his cane.

"Hello," Kevin said.

"It's me. Goober." I swallowed my pride and used the nickname first. "Thanks for your call. I'd like to talk."

"You would?" Kevin sounded surprised. "Gene, you want me to come over?"

"No. I'm not at home." I hesitated, realizing I should have thought through what I was going to say. "I . . . um . . . I may still be in trouble. The man who held me hostage, he wasn't working alone. I need some help, Kevin, but I don't want to get you in trouble, too."

"Hey, man, whatever." His voice rose with excitement.

"Can you meet me at the library at five-thirty? The main one uptown?"

"Yeah. Need me to bring anything?"

"No. I'll be in the computer room. I'll explain everything."

"Okay."

"And Kevin?"

"Yeah?"

"Come a round-about way. You may be followed."

"Really? Cool."

I hung up. He hadn't called me Goober once.

The time had come for quick decisions. Walking along the streets to uptown Charlotte would expose me to a steady stream of traffic. I didn't want to be spotted by friend or enemy until I'd reviewed the computer disks and talked with my father. One route came to mind that avoided the car-jammed roads. A railroad track now used only by the Charlotte Trolley ran from the south end of the city to uptown. I was only a few blocks from the rail line and could reach it by back streets. Then I could walk the crossties unobserved and disappear into the crowded sidewalks of late afternoon as the bank towers emptied their workers.

I followed the rails into the center of the glass and steel skyline, thinking Kevin Ferris would have to be handled very carefully. I couldn't tell him about Jeanne or Mr. Weaver and the transplant conspiracy was too crazy on the one hand and too dangerous on the other. No, I wasn't going to give Kevin information that could get him killed. I had to come up with something that fit the facts Kevin knew, something that would explain why I wasn't going to the police.

With each step I took, from the first crosstie to the last, I struggled for a story he'd believe. As I walked through the library door and into the treasure trove of volumes and volumes of books, I realized I didn't need a complete story for Kevin. All I needed was to plant the seeds and he would help me grow a new theory. Those seeds were the murder of Jeanne Everston's father, a dying Mr. Chamberlain's words to me which I would alter, and the encoded computer disks. It was five o'clock. I had thirty minutes to discover the secret of the list and decide which part would be the best bait to enlist Kevin's aid.

Clusters of computer terminals were housed in a glass-walled sector in the center of the library. I spotted a vacant workstation in the back, away from the view of other users. The librarian logged me in and blocked out the one-hour maximum I could hold that particular unit.

The system prevented the importation of data onto the hard drive from any outside source because the library couldn't afford to have its computers vandalized by corrupting viruses. I hoped whatever was on the CDs I had taken from Mr. Weaver could be accessed without some program application unique to his own hard drive. Otherwise, the disks were worthless.

I inserted one at random into the CD drive. Two files appeared in the contents window. "Anti.xys" and "Pro.xys." The xys file extension was not familiar to me. I double-clicked on "Anti" and immediately received the prompt to load the proper application. The library's resident programs couldn't open the file. I repeated the procedure with the "Pro" file and got the same response. I ejected that disk and inserted another. This time a single file read "Trans.xys." Again, the computer demanded a special application to open it.

The third disk was my last hope, unless I wanted to break into Mr. Weaver's house and run the disks on his computer. "Clarity.exe" appeared on the screen. "Yes!" I exclaimed, momentarily forgetting my surroundings. "Clarity" meant nothing to me, but ".exe" signified an executable program, the software which should access the other two disks. I typed the word "clarity," hit enter, and the screen went blank. No fancy graphics, swirling animation, or enticing sounds entertained me. A plain gray box faded up with a cursor flashing in the center. Over it hung a word that sent my hopes tumbling. "PASSWORD."

A real hacker would have blasted right past that obstacle and found a backdoor into the program. My skills left me without any choice except to guess. Mr. Watson, my English teacher, said the average human vocabulary was 50,000 words. Assuming the password was a word and not a string of unpronounceable letters or a huge mathematical number, I faced a one-in-50,000 chance of getting it right. I had to think of a word that Mr. Weaver and Jeanne would choose. I tried "Jeanne," "Weaver," "Everston," "transplant," "donor," but the message "incorrect" kept flashing.

Somewhere in my head, I remembered talking to Jeanne about a password. Then, as if she were standing right beside me, I heard her saying "we are the password." She'd been at the elevator yesterday morning and I'd kidded her about asking for a password from the lecture attendees. She'd given me the question, "How do you tell a boy chromosome from a girl chromosome?" I'd thought about X and Y. And here the suffix of the data files was xys. "We are the password," Jeanne had said. "You pull down their genes." Was that a double joke because it really was a password? Genes. I typed the five letters, and instantly the gray box vanished, replaced by the single sentence: "INSERT CD FOR PROCESSING." I was in!

17

With the Clarity program running in the computer's RAM, I ejected the CD and replaced it with trans.xys. Immediately, an "open file" prompt appeared, listing trans.xys as the only choice. I double-clicked the cursor on the name and saw the same page from the National Organ Procurement Center's website Mr. Weaver had shown me last night in the hospital. I duplicated everything he had done, from decoding the list to bumping Katherine Thompson's name from the top of the recipient priority placement. Doing it myself, manipulating the data like Weaver, made me less sure of what was happening. The whole great conspiracy could be nothing more than this CD-ROM, created for one purpose—to make me think a conspiracy existed. Yes, a conspiracy definitely existed, but which one? A scheme that had kept Katherine from her new heart or a scheme that kept me drugged and locked in a barred bedroom? I looked for an answer on the other disk.

The Clarity program listed both pro.xys and

anti.xys as files to open. I chose anti.xys and the screen displayed a roster of decoded names. There must have been a thousand or more, many of them foreign and some of them lined out horizontally with AKA written between them. I'd looked at the Wanted Posters in the uptown post office often enough to know that AKA meant "also known as." Some of the names here were strings of aliases, but I couldn't figure any common link other than the heading "ANTI."

I continued to scroll down through the alphabetized list. "Lambert" leaped out at me. "Lambert, Jason." There were no aliases alongside. It had to be FBI Special Agent Jason Lambert. No way was I accepting the same name as a coincidence. I kept scrolling. The remainder of the list had some familiar sounding Smiths or Taylors, but no one who stood out as a person I actually knew. Then I saw "Matthew Vinton," AKA "Mickey Sanford," AKA "Sidney Chamberlain." Chamberlain, the man who killed Dr. Everston, and the FBI agent investigating the murder were linked together in a computer file. Why?

The pro.xys turned out to contain less than a hundred names. There on the first page, I read "Jeanne Bradford" AKA "Jeanne Everston." Down the list appeared "John Linsman," AKA "John Everston." The scene in the lecture hall flashed fresh in my mind. I realized what had been troubling me all this time, but I hadn't been able to pinpoint the problem. Now I could. Jeanne had bent over the prone figure of her father. She was not crying "Dad," or "Daddy," or even "Father." "John," she'd said. "John." Dr. Everston wasn't her father.

But if the conspiracy to sell transplant priorities and procure the matching tissue from living, healthy donors was a hoax, then why was Dr. Everston murdered? Could Chamberlain have been a religious nut after all? His name appeared on the "ANTI" list. Anti what? Reproductive research? Genetic engineering? The Institute for Fertility and Reproductive Studies wasn't an abortion clinic, and Jason Lambert appeared on the same list. Maybe a zealot would think God wanted him to stop the recombination of frog DNA, but not an FBI agent.

These thoughts flashed through my mind as I scrolled down the "PRO" list, searching for the final player in my drama. He didn't show up until "W." "WEAVER, RANDALL J." Three AKA identities shared his data line: "WALKER, ROBERT," "WILLIAMS, RAYMOND," and then "WEAVER, RANDALL J." again. His pseudonym trail returned to the first identity. Why was it listed twice? Maybe the final AKA for each entry represented the current one. These people changed names like others changed shirts.

I scrolled to the end and discovered three additional names under the heading "PROSPECTS." None of them had aliases. The first one knotted my stomach. "ADAMSON, EUGENE – Charlotte, North Carolina." The two other names, "KIM, JONG," and "OSTROVSKY, LECH," not only sounded foreign, but they came with attached addresses: "Seoul, Korea," and "Warsaw, Poland." Was I a "PROSPECT" to be harvested like Jeanne suggested? Were these other people also targeted to wind up as replacement parts somewhere around the globe? The idea of a worldwide inventory seemed ridiculous. And only three people. Not much of a stockroom.

I looked at the library clock. Twenty after five. Kevin could show up at any minute and I was more confused than ever. For his own protection, Kevin needed to remain ignorant of the computer disks. I returned to the anti.xys file, the one containing the names of both Chamberlain and Lambert. As printable pages, the list ran to nearly forty. Too much to send to the communal printer available to my computer. And the story to Kevin had to be plausible even if improbable. A forty-page document did not fit in with "facts" he would have to believe.

I highlighted two pages: one with Lambert's name and the other with Chamberlain's, then hit the print command. The spool icon showed the data in queue for the next available printing. I hoped I wasn't behind somebody's summer school term paper.

The CD drive was no longer required. I stuck the three disks back in my pocket and returned the computer to its initial settings.

A middle-aged man stood at the high-speed laser printer watching pages spew into the collection tray. He wore a gray business suit and carried an alligator attaché case at his side. I wondered why he didn't have a secretary and computer in a fancy office somewhere forty stories above Tryon Street.

I looked around him and saw "EXECUTIVE CAREER CHOICE" as the heading on the printing pages. He was online job-hunting, after hours and out of the office. Fortunately for me and unfortunately for him, there weren't many options available. With only three sheets in the tray, the printer stopped. The man started to pick them up, then hesitated as the printer began again. My list emerged upside down.

"Excuse me," I said, reaching my arm between him and the paper. He had already twisted his head to scan the names, but I placed my hand directly over the sheet. "I believe this is mine." I yanked it free before it fell on top of his pages and kept my hand positioned for the next one.

"Young man," he said. "You're in my way."

"I'm sorry," I replied. "The system seems to have printed my job prospects in the middle of all of yours."

The second page came out of the printer and I pulled both close to my chest.

His face turned red.

"I wish us luck," I said. I meant it.

Turning away from the printer, I saw Kevin Ferris entering the main door from Sixth Street. He didn't look in my direction because the location of the circulation desk forced him to walk the opposite way until he could loop around those waiting in line to check out. Quickly, I folded the two sheets of paper in half, then half again. I unfolded and re-folded them a second time, adding additional creases. I didn't want the pages to seem freshly printed. I tucked them in the front pocket of my jeans and started looking at a shelf of software programs just inside the entrance to the computer room.

"Don't turn around." The mumbled whisper came from behind me. Kevin was in secret agent mode, pretending we didn't know each other.

I didn't reply and kept on sorting through the shelf.

"Well?" Kevin whispered.

"Well what?"

"Well, what should I do now?"

"I'm going to the Carolina Room. Come to the back in five minutes." I wandered away without saying another word.

The Robinson-Spangler Carolina Room was a special section on the third floor and contained books about the Carolinas and works by North and South Carolina authors. A reference librarian supervised the use of the collection. None of it could be checked out. Last spring, I'd spent several days researching the regional impact of the Civil War and discovered I could read at a desk behind the stacks and go unnoticed for hours. One night, the librarian even had to wake me up. If she hadn't had to shelve a book in my section, I might have spent the night locked up with literary ghosts. I knew the chance of anyone seeing Kevin and I together was extremely remote, especially since school wasn't in session and our classmates had neither a desire nor reason to hang out among the old volumes.

I looked into the room before entering. The librarian stood with her back to me, bending over the desk to help an elderly man in an orange and green Hawaiian shirt find a listing in the computer. I walked in and arced to the right so I faced away from them until a seven-foot-high row of shelves blocked their view. I pulled a book at random and went to the back corner where my customary table was empty. There wasn't another person in sight.

If I had tried, I couldn't have found a more boring book in the entire collection. *North Carolina Textile Production: 1850 – 1880*. The copyright was 1903 and the print seemed to have shrunk with age. If Kevin waited too long, he'd find me face down, drooling on the pages in an unconscious stupor.

"Gene?" He whispered my name as he peeked around the corner of the closest stack.

"I found it," I said, holding up the book. "It's fascinating. All the mill outputs for thirty years." If anyone overheard us, we sounded like two history geeks salivating over obscure trivia.

Kevin sat down at the table beside me. He wore faded blue jeans and a T-shirt stamped "BUBBA'S FISH CAMP – If It Ain't Fried, It Ain't Food." And he had the nerve to call me Goober. Kevin was only about five-foot, six-inches, and wiry like a stretched spring. He fidgeted, constantly shifting in the chair. His fingers drummed the table with anxious anticipation.

I took my time before asking calmly, "Are you sure you weren't followed?"

"No way, man. It was just like in the movies."

"This isn't a movie." I didn't mention my own movie trick of sliding the paper under the bedroom door to catch the key. I didn't want to encourage Kevin to do something stupid just because he saw Tom Cruise make it work.

"No, really," he said. "I took the white whale, that's Moby Dick, the old station wagon I drive. I went out to I-77 and headed south, away from town. I stayed in the passing lane until I came alongside an eighteen-wheeler, then I slowed to match his speed. We went like that for about a quarter mile. Other cars started riding my bumper, but I waited until the next exit was right on us. I sped up, cut in front of the tractor trailer, and headed straight up the ramp before anyone who might have been following me could switch lanes. I looped out to the airport and then back in through the west side. The car's off the street. I parked in the deck on Seventh and walked over."

"Good job," I had to admit. "But I don't want you doing any more stunt driving, Kevin."

"We'll do what we have to." He sounded tougher than his scrawny frame could deliver. "So who do you think may have been following me?"

"I don't know and I don't want them to get close enough to find out."

"This guy who tried to shoot you, he wasn't working alone?"

I started mixing fiction with fact. "He had a gun to my head. I was the hostage to get him outside. Maybe there was a car and driver waiting." I paused and decided there was one truth I wanted to set straight. "I didn't faint, Kevin. I got a signal from the security guard and dropped to the floor. The guard shot him."

"Unbelievable. I'd have fainted."

"I was plenty scared. So scared I never noticed what the gunman stuffed in my pocket." I pulled out the two sheets of folded paper and placed them on the table. "I found these last night as I got undressed in the hospital."

"What are they?" Kevin's voice crackled with excitement.

"Part of a list of names. There must be more because the alphabetical continuity is broken. I think the gunman was afraid he'd be captured with the list on his person. He must have transferred it while he held me."

Kevin hadn't ventured to touch the papers, but his eyes were fixed on them. "You think they're the people in his secret society?"

"I don't know." I unfolded the pages, set the top one between us, and pointed to Chamberlain. "But here's his name, or at least the name the police have given out."

"Why didn't you give this to them?"

"Because the FBI is involved."

"So?"

"The agent who interrogated me, who convinced the hospital to report I fainted and was under observation, that agent is named Jason Lambert." I pulled the top sheet clear and let Kevin's eyes run down the second page.

"He's on the list," he cried. He pointed to it like I'd never seen it before. "Jason Lambert's part of the conspiracy."

"And I don't know who to trust." I took the paper away from Kevin. "The less you know, the better."

"What about the Charlotte police?"

"Do you think they can keep me safe from an FBI agent? And this list doesn't prove anything."

"What are we going to do?"

"I appreciate the we, Kevin, but the safest thing's for you to have as little to do with me as possible. My dad's in Chicago. I'm calling him at seven tonight. If he can get me a ticket, I'll fly up there. I may need you to drive me to the airport."

"Sure, if you don't mind being seen in the white whale."

"The airport may be Greensboro or Columbia."

Kevin nodded, understanding my desire to avoid the Charlotte terminal.

"I'll ask my dad to wire money for gas," I said.

"No problem. I got paid last Friday. We can get wherever."

"Where're you working this summer?"

He pointed to his T-shirt. "Actually, I work at Bubba's year round. It's okay."

I realized I'd never seen Kevin at after-school activities. Maybe he had to have the job. I sensed there was more to him than wiseguy insults.

"Have you talked to Jeanne Everston?" he asked. "That's tough about her dad."

"Yeah, it's tough. But I haven't seen her," I lied. "Expect she's got a lot to deal with." Like tracking me down, I thought.

"And you probably want to stay clear of her. Not get her involved either."

"I plan to keep as far away as possible."

"I hope it doesn't cause a problem between you two." Kevin looked serious. There was no mocking sneer on his face.

"What are you talking about?"

"You and Jeanne. Everybody knows she likes you and you'd be crazy not to feel the same way." Kevin broke into his sly grin. "I mean, let's face it, you're not what I'd call a hottie. I couldn't believe she asked me to trade seats."

"In History?"

"Yeah. Wallingford never cared where we sat. After that first day Jeanne joined the class, she caught me in the hall and asked if I'd give her my seat. Sure. Who could say no to that face? Then I noticed her eyeing you in and out of class. That's when you weren't panting over her."

"Kevin, there's nothing between us."

"Okay, whatever you say."

I let the subject of Jeanne drop, but I believed him. She had started sitting next to me after Kevin moved to the back of the classroom. What else had I missed?

"Are you going to telephone your dad from here?"

"Yes, from a payphone."

"It's six now. What should we do in the meantime?"

"I'd better stay in the library. If you want to leave and come back, that's all right."

"When did you eat last?"

I had to think. Breakfast at Mr. Weaver's. "Breakfast at the hospital," I said.

"Why don't we go to the Rock Bottom Restaurant around the corner? I'll spring for sandwiches. Then you come back here while I fill up the car. You'll call your dad, make a plan, and we'll be ready."

The mention of food triggered the pain in my empty stomach. "That's the best idea you've ever had, Kevin."

The tension of the last two days eased as Kevin and I sat in front of giant cheeseburgers. We joked about school and talked about plans for our senior year. Kevin wanted to get his grades as high as he could, but go into the military rather than straight to college. He said his rich Uncle Sam was the best way to get tuition. It was nearly seven when we split up outside the restaurant. Kevin headed for Moby Dick and I returned to the library to call Dad.

The hotel operator connected me to his room. He didn't answer. After what seemed like an eternity of rings, the voice-mail activated. "Dad. I'm at a payphone. I'll call back in fifteen minutes." Maybe he had gone straight to a business dinner; maybe he was just running late. I couldn't keep calling every fifteen minutes. I would run out of change. I decided to call our home machine. Perhaps he'd gotten my earlier message but had a conflict at seven. He'd tell me how to reach him.

There was one new message at 4:55 P.M. "Mark? This is Nancy. Mr. Clifford's secretary called from Chicago. They wondered why you didn't show up for the three o'clock meeting this afternoon. They thought maybe you'd flown back here to be with your son. Please call as soon as you get in." Nancy was my dad's administrative assistant. He would have told her if he was coming back early. And the Sheraton in Chicago still had him registered as a guest. My legs turned to jelly. I reached out and held onto the payphone for support.

Someone had kidnapped my father.

THE PRESENT

18

I have often thought about that moment. I can't remember a time when I felt more alone. In some ways, it was tougher than when my mother died. Although you're never entirely prepared for the loss of a loved one, I'd known Mom's death was coming. But my father was my anchor, my safety net to get me out of a mess where there seemed to be no other way to escape.

Each of us comes to a time in our life when self-reliance is forced upon us in an overwhelming tide. There are smaller ripples which raise our maturity level: doing what we feel is right even if it's not cool, not tearing others down to build ourselves up, and learning to be judged by what we say and do rather than what we wear or drive. This is the process of growing up to be independent, but to suddenly realize there is no one else to turn to other than ourselves is the moment that tests everything that has gone on before.

As if it had happened only yesterday, I remember

how strength surged up from somewhere inside me. It was a strength others had given me. I wasn't alone after all. A part of me was my mother, my father, my teachers, my friends, all those who had shaped and supported me. I carried them with me then just as I carry them with me today. I was no longer afraid for myself, and I was determined to fight back for my father. As the strength flowed through my body, so did the certainty that he hadn't been harmed. It was me they wanted, and he was the bait to lure me.

I understood as I stepped away from the phone, that . . .

THE PAST

19

. . . Randall Weaver had orchestrated the disappearance of my father. Last night, I'd told him Dad was staying at the Sheraton. I'd escaped this afternoon, and within an hour, my father vanished. The size of their web and the speed of their response staggered my imagination. Yet, I was a force to be reckoned with. And I had the disks in my pocket.

Kevin steered the giant Chevy station wagon toward the curb in front of the library. The 1970-ish car wore the battle scars of too-close encounters and blotches of mismatched touch-up paint that could have been anything from Sherwin-Williams to shoe polish. Braking to a stop, the vehicle rocked up and down on dilapidated shock absorbers, looking like a dying whale bobbing on the ocean's surface. Moby Dick indeed.

I grabbed the outside door handle and pushed the button. It refused to budge. Kevin leaned across the mammoth front seat and yanked the inside lever. The door swung open on rusty, screeching hinges.

"Sorry. Only opens from the inside." Kevin grinned. "Give it a good slam so you don't fall out when I go around a curve."

I climbed in and shut the door so hard all the windows rattled. Then I looked for the seatbelt.

"It's down there somewhere," Kevin said. "Don't get many passengers."

My fingers explored the crevice between the bench seat and back. I extracted wads of paper and other accumulated debris before reaching the metal buckle.

"What's the plan?" Kevin asked.

"The plan is to make a new plan." I snapped the seatbelt together like a knight cinching his armor. "My dad seems to have disappeared."

Kevin's brown eyes grew so wide they nearly filled his thin, narrow face. "Disappeared? Like missing?"

"Well, he missed a scheduled meeting in Chicago and didn't call in." I tried to keep my voice from quivering. "Maybe it's just coincidence and he'll leave a message on our home answering machine."

"Maybe this FBI guy Lambert had him picked up."

"I've thought of that. If so, then Lambert will have to reach me somehow. Probably also through the answering machine."

"He wants the list back, doesn't he? Trade your father for the papers?"

Kevin might have been partially right. I suspected it was Jeanne and Mr. Weaver wanting the computer disks. If Lambert weren't working with them, he wouldn't know I had the disks. But Kevin was correct in that Lambert had the resources of the FBI to get Dad so quickly. I considered going to Detective Drakesford of the Charlotte Police and telling him everything. Even if he could protect me from Lambert, could he protect my father?

"You can't go home," Kevin said. "Your house is probably under surveillance. You wanna stay with me? I don't have to work tomorrow."

My plan had been reduced to wait and see. I needed a place to wait. "That would be great, Kevin, if it's not a problem for your family."

"My family?" He sighed. "My family is one person. My grandmother. Ten minutes after you meet her, she'll forget you're in the house. You'll be better hidden than if the Feds buried you in the Witness Protection Program."

A horn honked behind us. I looked through the dirty back window and saw a policeman in a patrol car waving us to move on. Kevin stepped on the gas and left the officer in a haze of blue smoke.

"Do you want me to take a round-about way?" Kevin asked.

I slumped down in the seat as we approached the major intersection of Sixth and Tryon. "No. Just swing wide of the hospital and Dilworth neighborhood. You don't live there, do you?"

Kevin laughed. "Yeah, right. They'd probably harpoon Moby Dick if I even parked there."

Kevin made a quick left turn and headed straight through uptown. Early evening traffic flowed smoothly and within a few minutes, we were on the outskirts of south Charlotte. We'd gone about half a mile beyond the warehouse district when Kevin turned left into a maze of narrow streets connecting pockets of modest homes that had been built in the 1950s.

"I didn't see anybody follow me off South Tryon."

"Good." I sat up, no longer worried about being spotted. "Are we close?"

"Closer than close. We're here."

He beached Moby Dick on a cracked concrete driveway alongside a small, single-story, brick home. The bluish flicker of a television was visible through the sheer curtains of the front picture window.

"Let's go in the back. I don't want to scare my grandmother."

I followed him to an enclosed back porch whose screen door had been patched so many times it looked like a transparent quilt. We crossed through a narrow aisle between plant pots and bags of various fertilizers.

"My grandmother loves flowers. She spends most of her day tending her roses."

We stopped at the windowless back door while Kevin searched his key ring. "She watches *Wheel of Fortune* every night and sometimes she's in such a hurry to get in front of the TV she forgets to lock up." He twisted a key in the top lock, and I heard the deadbolt slide. "Good." He inserted another key in the doorknob, jiggled it a few times, and opened the door. He reached around the wall and flipped on the ceiling light.

At one time, the kitchen had been white. Now, the metal cabinets wore a dingy yellow tinge and the large porcelain sink displayed the veins of mineral deposits left by years of a dripping faucet. The linoleum floor was crisscrossed with paths worn into it by hundreds of footsteps from the sink to the ancient refrigerator to the gas-burner stove. Although the décor was no match for the designer-magazine kitchens of the expensive Myers Park and Dilworth homes, this one was every bit as spotless.

"Grammy," Kevin called. "I'm back. I've brought a friend."

We stepped across the kitchen and through an open archway into the front living room. A woman who must have been in her mid seventies sat perched on the edge of a hardback chair only about six feet from the TV. A collective groan came from the studio audience as the wheel sputtered to a stop on Bankrupt.

"Serves her right," mumbled the old woman to no one. "Greedy, greedy. She could have solved the puzzle."

Kevin's grandmother wore a light-weight, flowery-print house coat. Her thin, gray hair was pulled up in a bun about the size of a teed-up golf ball.

"Grammy?" Kevin repeated.

She seemed distracted by the interruption and reluctantly tore her eyes away from the screen. The wrinkles in her face deepened as she smiled at Kevin. Then, at the sight of me, she threw one hand over her mouth and turned away. With her other hand, she grabbed a glass from the square end table beside her. She was not quite quick enough to keep me from seeing the dentures soaking in the glass.

"Kevin, you should have told me you were bringing company."

"This is my friend from school. Gene Adamson. He's going to stay the night. We're working on a summer project together."

His grandmother removed her hand from her mouth and faced me. She nodded a greeting, but kept her lips tightly closed across her gums.

"We'll be back in my room. I'll have the phone."

Grammy nodded again and tried to smile at me without splitting her lips.

"A pleasure to meet you," I said, trying to keep a straight face at the poor woman's toothless predicament.

As we walked back through the kitchen, Kevin grabbed a cordless telephone from a charger on the counter. "In case you need to make some calls."

I didn't want to make calls that could be traced to Kevin's number, but I didn't argue with him. It was better that he answer the phone than his grandmother. If Jeanne grew desperate enough, she might start calling everyone in school looking for me.

"How's this phone listed?" I asked.

"It's not." Kevin grinned. "Grammy doesn't like getting sales calls. And the bill comes to her, Gertrude Neubaum. She's my mom's mother."

Kevin was thinking the same thing I was. How hidden would both of us be?

The layout of the house had the living room and kitchen at one end, a short hallway ending in a bathroom at the other, and two bedrooms on either side of the hall. Kevin's was on the back of the house, which meant I wouldn't have to worry about being seen from the street. His room surprised me. A single bed spanned the back wall, but aside from a dresser and closet, the rest of the space was filled with shelves of books, potted flowers, and trophies.

"Sorry," he said. "I don't have a chair in here. I'll get one from the kitchen."

He left me alone, perhaps so I could look around without him standing there wondering what I thought. I thought there was more to Kevin Ferris than I suspected. The trophies were not for sports or academic awards; they were for horticulture. Most of them went back to years when Kevin was in middle school. Several came from Polk County in the western North Carolina mountains where Kevin must have lived before moving to Charlotte. Two were "Best of Show" from the North Carolina State Fair in Raleigh. If Grammy had a green thumb, she had certainly passed it on to her grandson.

Kevin positioned the kitchen chair just inside the door. "You can have the bed. I've got a sleeping bag in the closet."

I shook my head. "I'm not throwing you out of your bed. Let's get that straight right now."

"Suit yourself. Just don't complain in the morning."

"I'm happy to be in a safe place." I walked over to the shelf displaying Kevin's awards. "These are great. You still compete?"

"Nah, I outgrew that stuff."

"Outgrew growing prize-winning flowers?" I looked at the seedlings sprouting from three pots on the shelf below the trophies. "Then these must be real late bloomers."

"It's just a hobby now."

"I'd think Charlotte would have a big garden club."

"Not for people like me," he said quickly.

"What do you mean? You won two state competitions."

"I mean it wasn't a high-society garden club. We had a 4-H program in Saluda. I'd be laughed out of school if I tried to start one at Myers Park."

I heard the bitterness in his voice. Kevin Ferris had transferred to our high school in the tenth grade. We had a student body of over twenty-five hundred. For all I knew, that may be larger than the whole town of Saluda. And 4-H was some hayseed club I heard about as a kid watching *Lassie* reruns. I understood why Kevin had an edge and kept a self-imposed distance. He was afraid of being rejected.

"Did you move here with your grandmother?"

"She's lived here for forty years." He sat down on the edge of his bed. I felt uncomfortable standing over him, so I went to the kitchen chair and turned it around so I could straddle the seat and lean forward against the back. I waited for him to continue.

"It was a car wreck," he said softly. "An eighteen-wheeler slid on a patch of ice. Mom and Dad were coming the other way around the mountain curve. They died instantly."

"I'm sorry, Kevin."

"Well, I guess we've been through it, haven't we? You losing your mom and now this with your dad."

"But to have to move. To leave your friends." I looked around the room with fresh eyes. The flowers and the trophies were a past he couldn't reclaim.

"I've got Grammy and school. Well, school's been all right. With my job, I don't have time for sports or clubs, but my grades are good. I guess that's the main thing."

He and I knew that wasn't the main thing. Hanging out with your friends was the main thing. Or it had been until Mom got sick. I felt guilty that I'd never made an effort to get to know him. A city high school is like any society. Some people set themselves apart as cool, most of us are in the middle, and then there are the misfits. Kevin had seemed awkward and out of place and his sarcastic barbs didn't help. That was the surface none of us looked beneath. Inside, Kevin held a lot of pain and had no one to share it with.

"Is there anything we can do tonight?" he asked.

I tried to think, but my mind moved with the speed of a garden slug. Only one thing was clear. "No. Someone will get in touch with me. Probably through voice-mail at home or a message at the Sheraton in Chicago. Maybe even at the hospital."

"A swap?"

I went with Kevin's lead. "Yeah. My dad for the list."

"How will they know you didn't make a copy? How will you know they won't doublecross you?"

"Good questions." I forced a smile. "You've got all night to come up with the answers." Now I felt like a garden slug who had just tumbled into a shaker of salt. I was whipped. "I'd like that sleeping bag now. Things will begin early enough in the morning."

A few minutes later, Kevin closed the door

behind him. It was only eight o'clock but too late for me to do anything except recharge my batteries. I nuzzled into the fuzzy lining of the sleeping bag and counted sheep. Maybe I made it to five.

20

Some internal switch went from off to on. I awoke, fully alert, anxious to confront whatever and whoever stood between me and my father. The only problem— it was five in the morning.

Silently, I slid out of the sleeping bag like a snake shedding his skin. The single window emitted only a hint of the coming dawn, leaving the room in murky shadow. I listened for Kevin's breathing but heard only my own. Reaching across the bed, I discovered the spread hadn't been pulled down. Kevin had slept elsewhere.

I found him in the kitchen. He sat at the table, his arms folded on the surface as a makeshift pillow for his head. The light rustle of his rhythmic breathing told me he was dead to the world. Sheets of loose-leaf notepaper lay scattered beside him. In the dim glow of the wall-plug nightlight, I could see Kevin had drawn sketches. I recognized an overview of the hospital grounds. He'd labeled the entrance to the main tower and marked some of the side doors as well as walkways and service alleys between adjacent buildings.

Kevin's memory for detail surprised me. The accuracy of the layout was as good as I could have done and I work there every day.

I shook him gently on the shoulder. "Kevin . . . Kevin."

He jolted awake, looking up at me as if I'd fallen from the sky.

"Gene?" A whispered question, then, "Gene!" louder as his mind cleared. "What time is it?"

"Early. Why don't you go to bed for a few hours. You're no help if you're a walking zombie."

"The hospital," he said. "Make the trade at the hospital." He started gathering up the sketches.

"How'd you remember all this?"

"I didn't. I drove over tonight. Parked a couple blocks away and walked the grounds."

"Why?"

"You said you hoped to exchange the list for your father. You'd want to do it in a public place with plenty of witnesses if you want to be safe."

I nodded in agreement.

"You know the hospital. We'll work out an escape route and a back-up. The construction of the new children's tower has blocked a lot of the regular streets." He pointed to his map. "Moby Dick and I can be waiting in the back off Garden Terrace. They'll have to go three blocks out of the way to reach us. We'll be away before they try anything funny. What do you think?"

I thought Jeanne probably knew the hospital even better than I did, but I couldn't tell Kevin I thought she was involved. Actually, she and Mr. Weaver may find that arrangement appealing. Kevin had hit upon a good proposal without knowing the full implications. "Okay. It's worth a shot. You're amazing, Kevin."

He smiled and I saw him differently. The sarcastic smirk I always read in his expression had vanished.

"You still need some sleep," I said. "Do you trust me with Moby Dick? I want to use a payphone they can't trace."

"Sure." He stood up and fished the keys from the pocket of his jeans. "You can't hurt her. Wake me up as soon as you get back."

It took a few turns of the ignition key before the engine in the old station wagon started. The indicator for the automatic transmission was permanently fused in Low so I had to carefully slide the gear lever into Reverse. The diameter of the steering wheel seemed twice that of my Toyota. Maybe the car was more ship than whale. I set sail on the pre-dawn streets in search of a payphone. I didn't dare return to the Circle K. Farther out South Boulevard, I spotted a bank of empty phones on the side of an all-night CITGO. I parked Moby Dick as a barricade against the passing traffic, left the motor running, and dropped my coins in the phone closest to the car.

There were two messages on the home answering machine. The first came last night at three minutes after seven: "Gene. This is Jason Lambert. I'm very concerned for your safety. Please call in. I've tried to contact your father in Chicago, but he hasn't returned to the hotel or been seen since lunch. Let's work on this together, Gene. Again, I'm at 202-555-0801. Call me, day or night."

And at five minutes past midnight this morning: "Gene. It's Jeanne." Her voice was calm and friendly. "Something you lost has been returned to me. I'll keep it safe until we can get together, say, the same place we met last. Sorry, I don't have room for any of our friends." She clicked off immediately.

The possibility that Lambert and the FBI had taken my father disappeared. I had no doubt as to what had been returned to Jeanne. She spoke in code words knowing as well as I did the line was bugged. She wanted me to show up at Mr. Weaver's house alone. And she didn't want anybody else who might be listening, Lambert or the local police, to know where she was hiding.

I went straight back to Kevin's. The windows were still dark. I killed Moby Dick's engine and coasted into the driveway. I quietly let myself in the back door and tiptoed down the hall. Kevin's grandmother was still asleep.

By now, the morning light was bright enough that I could see Kevin curled up on top of his spread. Like Katherine in the hospital, he appeared smaller as he slept innocently unaware of the world around him. I realized both he and Katherine had broken hearts.

Although Kevin asked me to wake him as soon as I returned, the sight of him sleeping so peacefully caused me to hold off. A few more hours would give him needed rest and me the time to think.

I lay down on the sleeping bag and as the birds began to sing, I began to plan my father's rescue.

21

We drove past Mr. Weaver's house just under the twenty-five mile per hour speed limit. I huddled on the floor in front of the passenger seat and watched Kevin steal a quick glance.

"See anything?" I asked.

"No. The garage door is down. Curtains are drawn across all the windows."

"Good. They're less likely to see you leave the packet. Park as soon as we're out of sight."

He stopped Moby Dick about half a block away. Grabbing a manila envelope from the seat beside him, he opened the door. "What are you going to say if someone looks in and sees you wadded up under the dash?"

"The same thing you'll say to whoever is watching you talk to an empty car."

Kevin whipped his head around to check out the neighborhood. "Nobody's watching me."

"Then I guess nobody can beat you back here, can they?"

He slammed the door and sprinted away. Kevin hadn't asked what he was delivering and I hadn't volunteered the information. All he knew was this was the house where I'd been taken.

The envelope contained one computer disk and a note that said the other two were to be exchanged for my father in the main lobby of Carolinas Medical Center at two this afternoon. Otherwise, I would take the remaining disks and my story to the FBI. I suspected Mr. Weaver wouldn't want them to fall into Agent Lambert's hands. I glanced at my watch. Ten A.M. Four hours should be adequate time for them to arrange to get my father to the hospital.

I'd given them the CD with the fake organ recipient web page and kept the decoding application and the lists which included Lambert, Chamberlain, Weaver, Jeanne, and me. I had a hunch those were the ones with the greatest value to Lambert and, therefore, the greatest concern to the people who held my father.

Kevin sprang into the car like a gunman fleeing a robbery. He threw the transmission in drive and we started forward before he could close the door.

"What'd you do? Stop for coffee?"

He grinned down at me. "Fast, huh? Maybe I should think about going out for track."

"They run in circles. We're definitely not going to run in circles."

"I know. So you want to get up now and assume command?"

I unfolded myself from the floor and crawled into the seat. "Let's find a new payphone."

There were only two rings before someone picked

up and said "Hello." I faltered for a second, then blurted out the one-sentence message I'd been prepared to speak calmly and distinctly: "Check the front door." I hung up before there could be a reply. No longer did I have any doubt about pressing forward with the plan. My father had answered the phone.

THE PRESENT

22

I often think back and wonder if there would have been any difference in the final outcome if I'd spoken to Dad. I certainly wanted to. But hearing his voice startled me out of my self-imposed script and I couldn't trust myself to keep emotional control. Others had to be listening and I only wanted them to retrieve the packet at the door, not make a judgment on my resolve.

There are times when I suspect my father could have swayed me, could have talked me into simply returning to Mr. Weaver's. I'll never know whether that would have been a preferable course of action. I do know a death could have been avoided, but still, the cost might have been higher in the long run.

I've made peace with what-ifs. We make our choices moment by moment and if our intentions are good, a few bad choices will be overwhelmed by the overall pattern that will define our lives. I chose to hang up on my father and that act convinced Jeanne and Mr. Weaver far better than any words that I meant business.

At the time, I didn't know for sure if they'd follow the rules I'd laid down. So Kevin and I were like the third little pig who made a date with the big bad wolf, but showed up early. I had set the swap for two o'clock, but . . .

THE PAST

23

. . . Kevin and I got to the hospital at one. My employee code enabled us to get into the parking lot closest to the emergency room. We circled until a space adjacent to the building became available. I went over the plan a final time.

"I told them to stand in front of the elevators where they can watch the entrance to the main lobby. At two, they'll be expecting me to walk through the front door. Instead, I'll come down from the Children's Hospital and step out of the elevators behind them."

"What if they're not there?" Kevin asked.

"I'll ride back up and come down again. If they haven't shown by two-fifteen, I'll return to the car and we'll go straight to the police."

"Good," Kevin said, a little too quickly. I think he believed I was getting in over my head.

"Either way, with or without my dad, I should be here no later than two-thirty. If I'm not, you make the call from the emergency room. But, Kevin, not a minute sooner."

"You're sure he'll be in his office?"

"No, but you stress it's an emergency and they'll locate him. Tell them Gene Adamson is in trouble and Detective Drakesford and only Detective Drakesford can help." I grinned. "You can throw in 'it's a matter of life and death' just like in the movies."

"That's not funny." Kevin's normally red face had gone pale. Where was his sarcastic humor when I needed it?

I took a deep breath and felt smothered by the muggy air in the car. "Kevin, you can't stay in here for an hour. You'll roast."

"It won't be so bad with the windows down. And look." He pointed to the skyline of the city.

In the distance, huge vertical billows of white clouds dwarfed the skyscrapers. A tinge of gray began to form beneath the massive thunderheads.

"Forecast calls for storms," Kevin said. "That'll cool things down."

"Great. I rescue Dad, then get struck by lightning."

"It'll aid our getaway. Who could follow us in a downpour? And Moby Dick loves the water."

I left him chuckling at his own joke.

I entered through the Pediatric Emergency Department. Early afternoon is normally quiet and only a mother and feverish child were at the admittance desk. I went through a maze of corridors to the back elevators and rode to the children's floor. Avoiding the nurse's station, I slipped into a stock room, put on a cleaning crew smock, and grabbed a bucket. The supply shelves offered cleaners and disinfectants.

I loaded three bottles of ammonia in the bucket for extra weight and returned to the back elevators. When the doors opened, I was relieved to see the interior empty. I set the bucket against the rubber door guard and waited. As the elevator shut, the bumper struck the pail and reopened the door. The sensors were lightly set to allow for crutches, wheelchairs, and gurneys that required more time to get on and off. I hoped the bucket would weigh enough for me to block the elevator door while I stepped into the main lobby to get my father.

It was twenty after one. I had forty minutes to spare. I took off the smock and folded it in the bucket with the bottles. Then I hid everything behind the storage room door where I could reach it quickly.

I decided to take one final precaution. I walked through the Children's Hospital to the main elevators without seeing any of the nurses who knew me. Alone, I rode one down seven floors to the lobby. I wanted a final check that no construction or cleaning crews had roped off any areas which could impede the exchange. I wanted to appear like a magician out of the blue, make the trade, and be back in the elevator with my father before his captors could follow.

The door opened and I stared into the face of Nurse Helen McBride. She held a glass of iced tea in one hand and a chicken salad sandwich in the other.

"Gene," she shouted, loud enough for even Kevin to hear behind the hospital. "Didn't they tell you Katherine's in Pre-Op?"

"Pre-Op?" I was both stunned at the question and anxious to get out of sight. I stepped back and motioned Nurse McBride into the elevator.

"Lunch." She held out the food as evidence. "I'll ride with you to the fifth floor."

I punched the button and relaxed as the doors closed behind her. "There's a donor?"

"Yes. Didn't you get my message?"

"I just arrived."

"She's so anxious to see you. She's excited and scared at the same time. I hope you can get in."

"What's the schedule?"

"You know we aren't told where the heart's coming from. The jet's return flight is estimated at two hours so that could be anywhere from Boston to Dallas. The helicopter's been sent to the airport to meet Dr. Jacoby when the plane lands."

"Did he harvest the heart?"

"Yes. He left this morning."

The elevator light blinked as we passed the third floor. Neither one of us said anything. We were both thinking of an unknown family who had lost a child and, in the midst of their unbearable grief, given another child the gift of life. I hoped today would always be little Katherine Thompson's new birthday.

The elevator opened and we headed down the hall toward Pre Op.

"I'll speak to Lisa Comer," she said. "Lisa's head nurse on duty."

Nurse McBride hit the oversized button that activated the double doors. As they swung outward, I looked at my watch. One-thirty. There should be time to visit Katherine and return to the seventh floor for the smock and bucket. I needed to be in the main lobby at precisely two.

Lisa Comer waved us past her desk to a row of glass-paneled rooms.

"I'll wait out here and eat my sandwich," Nurse McBride said. "Don't want to crowd them."

I could see Mr. and Mrs. Thompson through the glass partition. They stood at the foot of the bed. Dr. Kaufman, the other half of the surgical team, was also there. He leaned over Katherine, saying something. I supposed they were words of comfort. He and Dr. Jacoby were the link between her failing heart and the one heading to the Charlotte airport. All their skill would be necessary if Katherine were to wake up on the other side of the operation with a new life in front of her.

Dr. Kaufman stood up and gave Mr. and Mrs. Thompson a reassuring smile. My eyes moved to Katherine's pale face, now visible between her parents. She looked in my direction, but didn't see me. A glaze had muted the sparkle in her eyes, the sign that pre-op medication had begun to tranquilize her. I waved and she focused on my hand. Then she recognized me. I read her lips. "Goober."

Her parents turned around and Mr. Thompson winked at me. Dr. Kaufman came to the door.

"Gene, come in. I'm going on to O.R. You can visit for a few minutes."

I stepped in the room and felt at a loss for words. I wasn't alone. Mr. Thompson barely whispered my name. Mrs. Thompson only nodded. Emotions were too high to speak.

Katherine turned her head to me. "My big day," she said weakly.

"That's right, squirt. Your big day." I walked over to her bedside and reached out to touch her hand. "You're a tough ol' bird."

She grabbed my wrist and squeezed. "So you gonna sing or what?"

"Sing?"

"One song?"

There was no way I could say no. I started "Goober Peas." Katherine closed her eyes, but she did not relax her grip on my wrist. My watch ticked unseen beneath her palm. Time raced on, pulling both of us toward the most important moment in our lives.

I finished the last chorus and tried to pull away.

"Another," she whispered.

I looked at her parents.

"Would you?" her mother asked.

Her plea didn't matter. I couldn't walk away from a ten-year-old girl who may not live out the day. We went through "Puff The Magic Dragon," "The Marvelous Toy," and "Sweet Baby James." Each time I stopped, she would squeeze my wrist and say "another." And each time, I would sing a new song. After all, I'd promised her that when the day came for her transplant, I'd be with her.

There was a knock on the door. Nurse Lisa Comer stuck her head in. "We're ready to go to O.R. The helicopter will be arriving shortly."

Katherine released her grip. She was ready.

"You be brave," I said. "We've got a lot more

songs to sing."

"Gene, I love you."

"I love you, too. I'll see you right out of recovery." I bent down, kissed her forehead, and left quickly without looking back. It was five minutes till two.

As I walked down the Pre-Op corridor toward the double exit doors, Nurse McBride intercepted me. "They'll be keeping the seventh floor posted on the progress. Dr. Kaufman expects the operation to last five or six hours."

"I'll be back."

"I'm glad I ran into you. I'd hate for you to have gotten the message on your machine after the surgery was over."

The hair stood up on the back of my neck. "Machine? I thought you left the message upstairs."

"Yes, but none of us knew when you were coming in. We were told you were taking some time off after that horrible shooting."

"That's right," I mumbled. "Thank you." I moved numbly to the doors. A message on my home machine could have been intercepted by anybody. I stepped out of Pre-Op.

"Well, Gene, I've been expecting you." Agent Jason Lambert appeared at my side. His hand was buried in his suit coat pocket. He lifted it just enough for me to see the top of the pistol. "We need to talk."

Up close, Agent Lambert didn't look much older than me. Except for his eyes. They glinted like hard blue ice.

"There's an empty family waiting room down the

hall," he said.

Time seemed to stretch and contract simultaneously. My mind raced while everything around me slowed down. Lambert nudged me and I started walking like mud sucked at my heels. Right now, Jeanne and Mr. Weaver should be bringing my father into the main lobby. How long would they wait?

"I'm expected elsewhere in the hospital. Nurse McBride will start looking for me."

"And she may never find you if you don't cooperate."

The mud grew deeper and my knees weaker. "I've written everything down and left it with a friend. If anything happens to me, the whole story will come out. I saw your name on the list."

Lambert stopped and I edged a step away. "So you know," he said.

"I know there are two groups. You and Chamberlain are in one."

"I suppose they've told you we're evil, bent on enslaving the mortals."

I couldn't mask my surprise. "Mortals?"

The ice-blue eyes pierced my forehead. "You don't know, do you? They haven't taken you into their confidence at all. Did you see your own name? What list are you on?"

"I'm a prospect. A potential donor, I guess."

It was his turn to look surprised. "Donor? You think this is about organ transplants? A list of donors?"

"Yes. Isn't it? They told me about a conspiracy to manipulate the priority cases, but I don't understand if that's really—"

He interrupted me. "Brilliant. A brilliant deception. They've brought you in while keeping you in the dark. Fed you a theory to fit the evidence."

I just stood there. I had no idea what he was talking about.

"You told me Chamberlain said you were on the list," Lambert said. "What did he say? Think again about his exact words."

I remembered laying my ear close to the dying man's lips. "The list," I repeated. "You're on the list. God's chosen, Gene."

Lambert nodded. "Gene, listen to me. Chamberlain was not saying your name. He meant gene as in chromosome. God's chosen gene." The FBI agent stepped so close I could feel the breath of his whisper. "We are the Eternals. And you may be one of us. You may live forever."

24

This man is crazy, I thought. He's an FBI agent, he has a gun, and he's nuttier than a pecan pie. I knew there was no way to argue with him. He might just shoot me if I said the wrong thing. "Forever?" I repeated.

"Yes. I'm glad they haven't poisoned your mind. You'll understand why we have to stop them. They are endangering all of us." He nudged me forward again. "Let's go to my car. There's too much to tell you here."

He directed me to a door beyond the elevators and into a stairwell. Silently, we descended to the ground floor without meeting anyone. Emerging into an empty hall, we started walking to the emergency room, the very exit route I'd planned to take with Dad. Perhaps Lambert had parked where Kevin could see me. Perhaps Kevin would call Detective Drakesford immediately or follow us. These perhaps were too slim to count on. Once Lambert got me in his car, all hope would be gone.

At the end of the corridor, the double doors flung

open. A rolling gurney sped toward us, flanked by a trauma team. "Clear the way! Clear the way!" yelled a resident leading the pack.

I pushed back against Agent Lambert. I could see bright red blood seeping through the bandage covering the patient's head. I couldn't tell whether the approaching victim was a man or woman. I glanced at Lambert. His gaze was riveted on the bleeding body. As the group passed, I jumped in front of them and sprinted ahead, leaving Lambert stunned and blocked by the gurney between us. I made it to the stairwell. Fear gave me a shot of adrenaline that boosted me up the steps two at a time. I ran by the second floor landing, hoping to gain more distance before exiting. If I could make it to the seventh floor, the Children's Hospital, I'd be on familiar ground.

Below me, I could hear Lambert's rapid footsteps. I passed the third floor landing. Breathing became painful and my legs felt heavier. Lambert sounded closer. Still, I pressed upward.

On the fourth floor, I found a laundry cart blocking the landing. Someone had set it out from the hall. Dirty towels and sheets overflowed its canvas sides. I wriggled past it, then turned and shoved the whole thing down the stairs. Lambert rounded the bottom as the cart rumbled down like a linen avalanche. Its weight knocked him to the concrete and he disappeared beneath a pile of tangled laundry.

I didn't risk another second. The seventh floor and safety were only three flights up. I took off again. At the fifth floor landing, I heard Lambert throwing the cart aside and continuing the pursuit. But I would make it and I would find someone who would believe me and protect me from this Federal maniac. I reached the sixth floor and the stairs stopped.

I had forgotten the operating rooms were in a tower wing that was not as high as the main hospital. I couldn't get to the seventh floor directly. I pushed open the door and stepped not into a hallway, but outside. The wind whipped my hair and a splash of rain struck my forehead. I looked out at the skyline of Charlotte.

The tops of the buildings were being devoured by black clouds. Streaks of lightning carved the heavens into ragged pieces of a jigsaw puzzle. Against this ominous background, a white dot grew larger. The medical helicopter raced ahead of the storm, fighting to gain the safety of the landing pad on the roof where I stood. I knew Dr. Jacoby would be seated by the pilot, clutching the cooler that held Katherine's life, counting the minutes until they would land.

This rooftop was also the end of my race. I couldn't retreat down the stairwell. To my left were ducts and air-conditioning units supplying ventilation to this wing. Beyond them rose the unfinished sides of the new Levine Children's Hospital. The workers had abandoned their exposed construction platforms for shelter below.

To my right was the helicopter pad. Without thinking, I ran across the marks of the landing circle to a storage locker on the far edge. Beside it, a six-foot mast held a windsock aloft. The orange tube whipped in multiple directions. I feared the chopper might not be able to land in the wild gusts.

A waist-high guardrail offered the only protection from the ground six stories below me. I wedged between the locker and the barrier, hoping Lambert would first search behind the air-conditioning units before crossing to this side. Rain fell harder. I dared not look around from my hiding place lest Lambert spot me.

The roar of the incoming helicopter overwhelmed the rumble of thunder. Wind beat down on me from the rotating blades. I looked up to see the belly hovering above me. The pilot swiveled to face the wind and gently lowered the craft. Dr. Jacoby's face pressed against the door window. He prepared to jump out as soon as they touched down.

As the helicopter descended, I stood up. The transporter of Katherine's life would have to be the salvation of my own. I looked for Lambert. He was at the far end of the roof, standing behind a cooling unit. Our eyes met for a second and we both started running.

Dr. Jacoby emerged from the cockpit with the cooler. He looked at me in astonishment, but swiftly took his precious cargo away. I climbed up into the chopper. The pilot yelled something which was swallowed by the engine. I pointed behind him and he turned to see Lambert running toward us. As the agent passed Jacoby, he pulled the gun. The pilot looked back to me, eyes wide. I frantically motioned for him to lift off. He revved the engine and concentrated on getting us airborne. I saw Lambert flip open his FBI shield with his free hand, but the pilot was no longer watching him. As the helicopter surged skyward,

Lambert ran to the edge of the railing, waving the gun and badge in front of us. The pilot halted the ascent, hovering above the pad. Lambert had won.

A terrific blast of wind hit us from the side. The pilot wrestled with the controls as we gyrated around. I saw Lambert jump away from the rear rotor blades, spinning knives that could decapitate in a heartbeat. The helicopter stabilized, but not before Lambert had flung himself against the guardrail with such force he toppled over it. For a split second, he hung in the air with us, suspended between earth and sky. A flash of lightning blinded me and then Lambert was gone.

25

The pilot managed to set the helicopter down on the pad and lash its struts in place. I ran down the stairwell without waiting for him.

Agent Lambert's body lay crumpled in a garden of pansies. A small crowd braved the storm to gather around. A medic bent over him, but there was no urgency. Lambert was definitely not immortal. Hospital security arrived less than a minute after I did. They started to clear people away, but the pelting rain was more effective than their orders.

"This man's an FBI agent," the medic announced. He held up the badge, then reached over in the blossoms and retrieved the gun.

"He was after me," I said. "Someone call Detective Carl Drakesford in the Charlotte Police Department. I'll only talk to him."

"Gene, what are you saying?"

I turned to face Billy McKay, the security guard who saved me from Chamberlain only two days earlier.

"I want a room where I can be alone until Detective Drakesford gets here." I pointed to the helicopter moored above us. "The pilot can tell you what happened. I'll tell Drakesford why."

As Billy McKay and another guard escorted me toward the door, I saw Kevin standing by the corner of the building. His sopping red hair hung down like mop strands and his eyes were big as doughnuts. I gave him a slight wave of my hand, signaling him to get away. There was nothing he could do for me now.

They put me in a waiting room off the CATSCAN diagnostic suite. I sat in a blue plastic chair, staring out the window, watching the storm die. Behind the steel-gray edge of a trailing storm cloud, half a sun sent sparkles shimmering through the final drizzle. I knew somewhere there was a rainbow. Somewhere.

Outside the door of the room, a hospital security guard probably gave no thought to rain or rainbows. I was under house arrest, or more accurately, hospital arrest.

There was a knock. I turned from the window, hoping Detective Drakesford had made it in record time. I just wanted to get everything over with.

The door opened. My father walked in.

Suddenly, I was five years old. I ran to him, unashamed to wrap myself around him. He hugged me fiercely. In my ear, he whispered, "Lambert didn't tell you anything. You don't know why he was chasing you." The two sentences were not questions. They were statements. They were instructions in a voice commanding me to obey. "He didn't tell you anything," my father repeated.

"I don't know why he was chasing me," I whispered back like some responsive ritual in church.

"Good." My father placed a hand on each of my shoulders and pushed me back to where we stared eye to eye. He looked every one of his forty-four years. The gray seemed to have grown in his hair overnight. Then he said the strangest thing and I saw tears in his eyes. "Don't ever forget your mother."

"I won't, Dad. Ever."

He smiled and a moment passed, a moment he understood and I didn't.

"How did you get—"

"Here?" he interrupted.

I was going to say "away," but I let him continue.

"Your friend Jeanne and I ran into a boy named Kevin. He told us about the accident and that you were waiting on Detective Drakesford. I insisted hospital security let me see you."

"And Jeanne?"

"She's gone on. She was very helpful."

I didn't know if we were playing some kind of game because the security guard stood within earshot. Had Dad or had he not been kidnapped? It was true that if Kevin saw Jeanne, he would have spoken to her. I'd never mentioned her involvement to him. Kevin knew Jeanne worked at the hospital. When she introduced my father, Kevin might have thought the exchange had been made successfully before Lambert's death and that Jeanne and my father knew each other. But it was obvious Dad didn't want to answer any questions now. That was fine. All that mattered to me was my father was safe. I'd follow his lead.

"Mr. Adamson?"

Detective Drakesford stood in the doorway. He looked at my father and then at me. His face was all business. Police business.

"Yes," my father said.

"Carl Drakesford. We spoke on the phone Monday."

"Detective Drakesford, what's going on here? Why was that man chasing my son?"

My father's outburst surprised me. He never lost his temper, even mildly. If he was trying to put the detective on the defensive, he failed. Drakesford simply pointed to the chairs.

"Why don't we sit down and find out."

For the next twenty minutes, I played dumb. I only said what could be checked out: Nurse McBride left me a message about Katherine Thompson's transplant because I'd promised to visit her before the surgery, Kevin Ferris gave me a ride since I'd been staying with him till my father returned, and I left Pre-Op and started for the roof to watch the helicopter come in when Agent Lambert stopped me in the hall.

Drakesford made me go over that part again. "He didn't say why he wanted you to go with him?"

"No. It wasn't like he put me under arrest. He said he wanted me to get in his car. He showed me his gun."

"In his shoulder holster," Drakesford stated as a

fact.

"No. Hidden in his suit coat pocket. He had it out of the holster. That seemed strange."

Drakesford didn't comment, but I could tell from his face he didn't like the idea.

"Then the trauma team burst through the door. I just wanted to get away. To talk to you. You told me we were on the same team." He nodded as I gave him back his words. "I guess Agent Lambert scared me. I'm sorry. If I hadn't run, he'd still be alive." My voice broke as it hit me. He'd still be alive, but I might not be.

Drakesford rubbed his wide hand across his shaved dark scalp. Then he stood up and looked out the window. "I'm not saying this, understand? Lambert was a loner, even for a Fed. I got the feeling there was more to this case, a lot more, than he was sharing. He was way off base, pulling a gun like that. There'll be an investigation, but I bet it will center more on Lambert than you, especially if everything you've said checks out."

"I've got no reason to lie," I lied.

Drakesford turned around. The afternoon sun, now free of the clouds, created a golden halo behind him. I squinted at the dark angel.

"You and your father need to stay in town. There'll be questions. Not from me, but from the Bureau. I'll give you one word of advice—cooperate. Now, you're free to go."

We said goodbye and my father was overly gracious to make up for his initial reaction. We walked down the hall in silence. I could feel Detective

Drakesford's gaze following us until we turned the corner.

"What happened, Dad?" I whispered.

"Wait till we're in the car."

The car was my Toyota, parked in the Visitor's deck. Dad pulled the keys from his pocket. "Drive us home."

I paid the parking attendant two dollars and soon joined the light flow of traffic moving out of the city an hour ahead of the five o'clock rush.

My father began answering my unasked questions. "When we broke for lunch yesterday, there was a sealed envelope waiting for me with the secretary outside the conference room. Inside I found a single sheet of plain white paper on which someone had neatly printed 'Say nothing to anyone. Do not contact the police. Gene is in trouble. Use this and look for Dr. Baker.' Clipped to the note was a one-way airline ticket from Chicago to Charlotte. The flight left O'Hare at one-thirty. I had less than an hour to get there."

"Did the secretary say who delivered the envelope?"

"An employee from the mailroom. Evidently, a man walked in, handed over the envelope and said I was expecting it."

"Who was Dr. Baker?"

"Words on a sign carried by Randall Weaver. He was standing at the gate when I arrived in Charlotte."

"Dad, he held me prisoner in his house. Did he tell you that?"

"Yes. And they'd purchased my ticket before you

escaped. He said they were protecting you from Jason Lambert. It looks like they had good reason to fear him."

"Why bring you back to Charlotte?"

"So they could explain everything to both of us. But you ran away before I arrived. They thought I was the only way to get you to come in. They didn't know where you were and they were afraid Lambert would bring the full force of the FBI to find you."

"You know what Lambert told me?"

"What?"

"He said he was immortal and that I was, too."

"I don't think so," Dad said.

"You got that right. Unless he can come back from the dead."

"I don't think he said he was immortal."

The tone in my father's voice pulled my eyes from the road. He sat beside me, staring straight ahead. For the first time, I noticed his wrinkled suit and shirt. He probably hadn't slept in thirty-six hours.

"He said he was an Eternal, didn't he?"

I looked back to the road. Only another mile till we'd be home. I heard my blood pounding in my ears. "Eternal." That was the word Lambert had used. I was scared. The unknown had opened up as a chasm between me and all that was familiar. My father sounded like a stranger.

"And he said that you might be one of them."

"Yes," I said. "He was crazy."

"He may have been crazy, Gene. And he may have been telling the truth."

I turned into our neighborhood, letting the silence

hover between us. They might have drugged him, hypnotized him. I should have suspected as much. Maybe we should never have left the hospital. I'd get him into bed, then call Kevin to get our story straight on how he and I had just hung out for a couple days. After my father rested, we'd start over and make sense out of Lambert, Weaver, and Jeanne. There had to be a rational explanation.

Our house was a traditional two-story brick with a small front porch. I pulled in the driveway and stopped at the front walk. Normally, I parked at the end of the driveway and went up the stairs to the back deck, but I wanted to get my father inside as easily as possible. He seemed to move slowly getting out of the car. However, his stride was steady and he forced a smile to assure me he was okay. I walked alongside him to the front door. The key was in my hand. As I reached for the doorknob, it swung inward on its own.

I jumped back and my father caught me by the arm.

"It's all right," he said.

Jeanne Everston stood in front of me.

"Welcome home," she said.

26

I followed Jeanne into our living room like it was a formal visit to someone else's house. Mr. Weaver and the dark-skinned man I'd seen in Jeanne's Miata stood up from the sofa. They nodded to my father.

"Everything went fine," Dad said. "There'll be some inquiries. Routine."

"Wonderful," Jeanne said. She looked at me and smiled. She was so beautiful, so treacherous. And now my father was one of them. I half expected him to reach up and pull off his face, revealing some alien impersonator.

Mr. Weaver smiled at me. "Gene, it's time we had more honest introductions." He reached up to his own face and tugged at a wrinkled cheek. Flesh-colored adhesive peeled back to disclose smooth, unblemished skin. "I'll forego the rest of my makeup. You'd recognize me as the young Union soldier whose photograph you saw in my bedroom. The woman with me in both pictures was my wife Helen. In one, she is twenty. In the other, forty-five. I looked the same. I was born in 1846, fought at Gettysburg, and have taken several aliases before returning to my original name in 1945 when I re-emerged to enter the budding field of computer science. You may find this story fantastic, but I assure you it's all true. I understand quotes from my Civil War diary helped earn you an A in history."

I turned to Jeanne for an explanation.

"I'm only twenty-five. Jeanne Bradford. They found me seven years ago. Like you, I'd been typed as a potential organ donor for my mom."

"So that wasn't a lie," I said sarcastically.

"No, Gene, my mother died. But my tissue was flagged by an operative and I was evaluated."

I checked my anger. The pain in Jeanne's face as she remembered her mother was all too real.

"And you are?" I asked the young man.

He bowed from the waist with his hands clasped in front of him. "Now I am known as Vinay Patel," he said in a smooth, cultured voice. "Please call me Vinny."

"Vinny?"

He chuckled. "I know it sounds Italian, but I have a fondness for them. They were my first Europeans."

He appeared completely westernized. His English sounded perfect. He wore a light green cotton pullover and khaki slacks. A small gold chain encircled his neck.

"You're Indian?" I asked.

"Yes. I left that continent with Venetian sailors returning from Asia. Perhaps you've heard of Marco Polo?"

"Marco Polo?" I laughed. "You expect me to

believe you were born in . . ." I had to think for a
second, ". . . in the thirteenth century?"

"No, Gene. In the fourth century. I was already
nine hundred years old when I migrated west, joining
Polo as he stopped in India on his return from
Sumatra."

I shook my head. "Come on, Dad, this is ridiculous."

"I thought so, too," he agreed. "I'm not saying I
believe them. But they're only asking us to listen. Then
they'll leave us alone. Isn't that right?"

"Absolutely," Weaver said.

"No," I said. "I've already listened once. Listened
to their lies about corruption in the organ procurement process. They used deceit to lure me out of
the hospital."

"And what did you tell Kevin?" Jeanne asked.

"Kevin's got nothing to do with it."

"He was at the hospital this afternoon. It's easy
enough to figure out. He drove you there. He's been
hiding you. Did you tell him about us?"

"Of course not. I was putting him in enough
danger just being with me."

"Exactly," she said sharply. "You probably said
just enough to explain the facts that you had to, which
is no more than we did to protect you. On the phone,
you told me Katherine Thompson had been passed
over for her transplant. Then you said Chamberlain's
dying words had been about a list, a list you were on.
Randall and I had to create, and create quickly, a
plausible story that would get you where we could
protect you." She looked to Weaver for reassurance.

"I put that computer program together in six hours," he said. "It perpetrated a conspiracy you could understand and one you would fight against for the sake of the little girl. Would you honestly have left the hospital if Jeanne had said she had a seventeen-hundred-year-old friend she wanted you to meet? And what if we'd revealed ourselves to you? You could have gone to Lambert. If you had, what makes you think you'd still be alive?"

I didn't answer. I couldn't answer. Lambert had shown me how far he would go.

"I think we need to sit down," my father said. "Especially if Vinny is as old as he claims. I'll start some coffee."

"Would you have green tea?" Vinny asked.

"I think that can be arranged." Dad left for the kitchen.

Vinay Patel and Randall Weaver sat on the sofa. I perched on the edge of one of the two matching armchairs, too nervous to relax. Jeanne took the other one.

"What did you mean you were evaluated?" I asked her.

"The tissue match flagged me as a prospect."

Prospect. I remembered my name had been under that same heading.

"We have someone with access to the databank who looks for one characteristic—stem cells."

"Stem cells?"

"Cells that can become any tissue," Jeanne said. "They are the cells of early embryos. Adults still have a few, but for some unknown reason, we carry a much higher level."

"You think that's what keeps you from aging?"

"We don't know for sure," Vinny answered. "This is new science to us, too. However, the evaluation isn't just of tissue, but also of character."

"Character?"

"Yes. That's why Jeanne's been observing you for the past five months. We can't afford to approach and reveal ourselves to someone who's not of high moral character. Knowledge of your unique status comes with a heavy burden." He looked at Jeanne and Mr. Weaver who nodded in agreement.

"Because you outlive your family, your friends?"

Vinay Patel answered with a string of unintelligible syllables. Then he said, "Those are words of my native tongue. A long extinct dialect of Sanskrit. They were shouted and spit at me by a mob of my kinsmen descending upon my home because they thought I was evil. Death to the Demon is a rough translation. An illness was sweeping through our village, young children were dying, and I was accused of sapping their life to stay young. I escaped within an inch of my life only because no one wanted to be the first to touch me. I disappeared into the lower castes, which is as close to becoming invisible as you could get. I thought I'd been cursed by God, doomed to be reviled by my fellow creatures."

"But you found others," I said.

"In 1484, I tracked the rumor of an old woman known as the Eternal One. She lived in a village in the Swiss Alps. Like me, she'd disguised herself, made herself appear older. She was only one hundred and fifty."

"What did you have in common?"

"Nothing, other than we didn't age. She was overjoyed to discover another of her kind. Through the centuries, a few more were added as folktales of our isolated existence drew others to us. We tried to live in secrecy. Gene, the burden you must bear is the inevitable hatred of others. I'm not talking about your father or older relations. They expect you to outlive them. But imagine how the ultimate prize—perpetual youth—is seen by those condemned to age and die."

Vinny looked at the back of his smooth hands. I imagined if he were telling the truth, he'd held countless hands he'd seen grow old and wither.

He looked back at me. "Only within the last thirty years have we begun to understand the genetic root of our existence. As scientists map the genome, they search for the aging gene, a switch that can be turned off and a fountain of youth that can be turned on. If that possibility exists in the laboratory, then why wouldn't it happen in the greatest genetic laboratory of all—the reproducing human population?"

"You mean the mutation would happen nature-ally?" I asked.

"We guess maybe one in every thirty to fifty million births. In the smaller populations of the past, the numbers of such mutants would be extremely rare. And wars, natural disasters, and other killing forces would decimate those genetic abnormalities along with everyone else. Now, as populations balloon and tech-nology provides accurate ways to identify and track citizens, we risk wholesale discovery. We didn't want

the bodies of Chamberlain and Everston to be examined. Chamberlain had eradicated fingerprints
which could be computer-enhanced to match those of
a man who died in 1959. That was a re-emergence."

"A what?"

"Re-emergence. The end of a life-span. A faked
death of an identity and the creation of a new, younger
one. I underwent my most recent three years ago. But
the databases are becoming so sophisticated, it's becoming more and more difficult to re-emerge. We're
trying to work our way into places of influence for our
protection. And we are trying to research the genetic
code, discover why we are who we are, and perhaps
offer longer life to the rest of humanity."

"So that's why Dr. Everston worked at the
Institute For Fertility and Reproductive Studies," I
said.

"No," Vinny said. "We do have a person in
genome research, but Dr. Everston was looking for
something else. There's a conspiracy, a conspiracy of
the genes. They've given us perpetual youth, but
they've taken away our ability to reproduce. It's as if
the species has protected itself against stagnation,
against being usurped by a strain that has no need of
offspring. We are all sterile."

Beside Vinny, Mr. Weaver sighed. He seemed
older than he had first looked, even with the patch of
ageless skin peeking beneath his makeup. I remembered the photographs: a young couple and then an
older woman and a young man. There'd been no
pictures of children in his room.

"And Chamberlain," I asked, "he and Lambert

were against this research? They were in the Anti group?"

"Yes," Jeanne said. "Most of the Eternals don't approve of our efforts. They're afraid. However, a small but extreme faction has now developed among them. They want nothing to do with plans that would someday reveal us to the rest of humanity or give us the ability to have children. These zealots believe only God chooses the Eternals and has destined them to rule, to eventually control all the institutions of wealth and power. The murder of Everston was a message to the rest of us."

"But if they're so worried about secrecy, why such a public assassination?"

Jeanne glanced first at Randall, then at Vinny. She was unsure how to answer.

"A very perceptive question, young man," Vinny said. "It was an unexpected action which caught all of us off-guard. Perhaps that's why they undertook it. I can only surmise that it served two agendas, the private one to eliminate one of our group and the public one to strike fear in all researchers who might make discoveries that could benefit our cause. They expected the murder to be chalked up to religious zealots."

"And they'd have the CDs," I added.

"Yes," Jeanne said. "Fortunately, Chamberlain wasn't able to pass them on to his colleagues. Lambert must have suspected your identity because of the words Chamberlain whispered to you. That's why he lied to Detective Drakesford about the phone call I made to the hospital playroom. He couldn't afford for the policeman to become suspicious about you, even though Lambert knew you knew he was lying. Maybe he thought you'd appreciate the deception and confide in him. Now that he's dead, your identity is safe—for now."

Dad came in with a silver tea tray. It hadn't been used since Mom died. I suspected he'd been standing in the hallway behind me, waiting for an appropriate time to enter.

"And you told my father all this?"

"Yes," Vinny said. "Everything except the possible consequences of Lambert's death." He looked up at my father. "We think your son is out of danger for the time being. Now that he's heard our story, it will be up to him to choose his own path."

"That's it?" I said. "You come into town, tell me I'm immortal and sterile, and ride off again?"

"No. I leave you a number to call day or night. If it ever changes, you'll receive another. Use it tomorrow or use it ten years from now. We want you to know you're not alone. Time will prove us wrong or right about what we've told you and about the kind of person we think you are."

"What kind of person is that?"

Tears formed in Jeanne's eyes. "A person who would be at the bedside of a scared little girl regardless of his own safety. A person who's lost someone dear to him and knows it's not how long you live but what kind of life you make for others that's important. I'm betting you are God's chosen, Gene."

"God's chosen," I repeated. "Who's to say what God has chosen? How can we live for centuries and have children and not overwhelm the rest of God's creation?"

"Because the time is coming, my young friend, when our gift will fulfill its purpose," Vinny said. "The rest of God's creation is awaiting us. We aren't meant to rule our brothers and sisters here on earth. We are meant to lead them across the voids of space normal lifetimes cannot span. That's why we have been chosen, why we have been prepared. We are Eternals in the sense that mankind is eternally exploring. Our genes will guide our species to the stars."

27

All but the brightest stars were obscured by the lights of the hospital. The moon had not yet cleared the eastern horizon.

I walked along the edge of Employee Parking Lot B. At a few minutes after eleven, the grounds were mostly deserted. Visitors were leaving by the front of the complex and the only people I saw were two security guards making rounds in a motorized cart. I waved innocently as I passed.

Two nights ago, I'd hurried along these back walkways with Jeanne, starting an adventure that was only just beginning. That seemed like a lifetime ago. Maybe not, if I had to re-define lifetime.

The three of them left Dad and me that afternoon after tea. I now carried a ten-digit phone number in my wallet. I'd chosen an identification password: "Goober." We would meet again tomorrow before Jeanne Bradford, Randall Weaver, and Vinay Patel disappeared for all our safety. My only instructions were to finish high school, to consider a career that could contribute to the cause, and to watch my back.

My immediate mission lay in the cardiac intensive care unit. Katherine Thompson had survived the surgery and her new heart beat strongly. She'd be drifting in and out of consciousness for the next several hours. I was determined to be there for at least one of those awakenings.

I found her family in the waiting room for the pediatric intensive care unit. Visitors were allowed for ten minutes once an hour. Mrs. Thompson gave me a hug and Mr. Thompson shook my hand. I wondered if they'd heard about what happened on the helicopter pad.

"Only two of us can go in," Katherine's mother said. "Richard will skip this next one."

I turned to Mr. Thompson. "You're sure?"

"She's seen me. She knows I'm here and she knows I'm a terrible singer."

We donned surgical masks. The individual intensive care rooms were laid out in a circle around a central monitoring station. The lights were kept low. Nurses and doctors worked calmly and efficiently.

Even in the dimness of the room, I could see the change. "She's pinker already," I told her mother.

"She's beautiful," Mrs. Thompson said. "Someone has given my little girl a future."

I reached out and lifted the dainty hand from the sheet. The fingernails had lost their bluish color. Blood flowed, bringing oxygen and nutrients throughout her body.

Her fingers wrapped around mine and her eyes opened. She whispered one word—"Sing."

THE PRESENT AND THE FUTURE

28

And so I sang and she closed her eyes for the last time. I laid her wrinkled hand back on the sheet. That was five years ago when Katherine's borrowed heart of sixty-six years finally stopped beating. For fifty-six of those years, Katherine Thompson had been my wife.

Her life was not particularly long, not by the standards of 2070 when most people live into their nineties or the first decade of their centennial. What matters is that we were happy. She knew life as a gift and that she'd been given that gift twice. She knew I am an Eternal and I will carry her love forever.

Now this part of my story is over. I re-emerged last year, 2075, as a twenty-five-year-old Swiss medical school graduate. Vinny's connections still run deep here. I'd been a doctor in genetic research in the States and the promise of greater longevity is attainable before 2100. Others will carry on that work. My only regret is leaving behind my best friend, Kevin. He's now eighty-eight and still making contributions to horticulture. I was godfather to his three children and

I will miss them.

Jeanne and I are together. She's as beautiful as the day I first saw her in Mr. Wallingford's history class. Katherine had hoped I wouldn't be alone. "Marry Jeanne," she told me.

The conspiracy of our genes has never been broken. We have no children of our own. The "Anti" faction continues to be a force vying for the loyalties of new prospects. These battles are for other books. This one will be sent anonymously to Kevin. Of course, the names have been changed, but the message is still true. We are all given one day at a time. How we live it is up to us.

As for Jeanne and me, our future is with the *Marco Polo*, the interplanetary exploration ship being constructed in Brazil. Randall Weaver will be joining us on the maiden flight next year. And the elderly Indian scientist heading the project assures us we are well qualified.